TOUGH SCORE

KENNA KING

Copyright © 2024 by Kenna King

All rights reserved.

This book is a work of fiction.

No part of this publication may be reproduced, distributed, or transmitted in any form or by any means, including photocopying, recording, or other electronic or mechanical methods, without the prior written permission of the publisher, except as permitted by U.S. copyright law. For permission requests, contact Bridgetown Publishing Inc at info@bridgetownpublishing.com

The story, all names, characters, and incidents portrayed in this production are fictitious. No identification with actual persons (living or deceased), places, buildings, and products is intended or should be inferred.

Book Cover Design: Star Child Designs

1st edition 2024

Contents

Book Order	V
Chapter One	1
Chapter Two	12
Chapter Three	22
Chapter Four	43
Chapter Five	52
Chapter Six	61
Chapter Seven	70
Chapter Eight	80
Chapter Nine	86
Chapter Ten	104
Chapter Eleven	112
Chapter Twelve	118
Chapter Thirteen	129
Chapter Fourteen	136
Chapter Fifteen	142

Chapter Sixteen	148
Chapter Seventeen	158
Chapter Eighteen	165
Chapter Nineteen	180
Chapter Twenty	192
Chapter Twenty-One	199
Chapter Twenty-Two	207
Chapter Twenty-Three	212
Chapter Twenty-Four	220
Chapter Twenty-Five	231
Chapter Twenty-Six	241
Epilogue	247
Backmatter	251

The Hawkeyes Hockey Series

1. Cocky Score

2. Filthy Score

3. Brutal Score

4. Rough Score

5. Dirty Score

6. Lucky Score

7. Tough Score

8. Perfect Score

9. Wrong Score

Check out **www.kennakingbooks.com** for more books and information.

SCAN ME

Chapter One

Keely

Walking down the hall of the Hawkeyes' main office, I follow Adel, the owner's assistant, as she leads me down to the General Manager's office. Adel is the same woman who sent me the acceptance email for my job application with the franchise and scheduled my interview with Sam Roberts.

It's far too soon to get my hopes up, especially since the reason I got this interview was because my uncle Oakley called in a favor to Penelope Roberts, the newly appointed Assistant General Manager, and the current GM's daughter. Still, the opportunity to interview for a Physical Therapist position for a professional sports team is a dream come true. It's the career I've been working toward and the reason that I went into sports therapy after getting my doctorate in physical therapy. I never dreamed I'd be in the corporate office of a professional sports team, due to my family's past. Especially after being let go from my last job.

"I heard that you're the niece of the team's favorite bar owner," Adel says.

She glances over her shoulder with a smile as if she knows my Uncle Oakley. I bet she does, considering that all of the Hawkeyes players buy a beer or two from him after every home game.

Up until I moved from Arizona to Seattle last week and started working for him part-time to earn my keep for staying in the studio apartment above his garage, I had no idea that my uncle's bar is the Hawkeyes' unofficial after-game hang-out spot. Last week, the team was out of town for their away games, but the fans all still showed up at Oakley's, decked out in Hawkeyes' gear. They gave me a small taste of what to expect after the Hawkeyes play a home game tomorrow night.

I assume that the reason I've never heard about the professional team that frequents his bar is because my uncle didn't want my father to know where he could have quick and easy access to a group of professional athletes. This is a tip my career-criminal father would have found useful about fifteen years ago. That is, before he went to prison for a decade and a half on racketeering charges for trying to pay off a soccer team to throw the World Cup for the mob.

Ever since the days of watching professional sports on the couch of my father's condo every other Saturday, per his visitation agreement with my mother, I knew at a young age that I wanted to be a part of this world. It didn't matter what was on: football, baseball, hockey, basketball, or golf, we'd watch it all.

The irony is that the man who brought me to my first love is also the man responsible for the six-month gap in my resume and the reason why I moved to Seattle from Arizona. I needed to get out of the city that knows too much of my family's dirty laundry.

He went away when I was in eighth grade and now at twenty-nine years old, I'm forced to start my life over again in a new city. After fifteen years, most of the world has forgotten about my father's trial. His name was buried under all the bigger names that were also on trial for the same bust. But it was a big deal in the community we lived in.

My dad was my t-ball coach, sat on numerous charity boards, and he was the head of our gated communities neighborhood watch. He was the kind of guy who would go out of his way to help anyone.

It took years after his high-profile trial for people in the city I grew up in to forget that I was Barrett Humphries' daughter. My mother even had my last name legally changed from Humphries to her maiden name—Woods. But it didn't matter. I grew up in that city so it only took days after the local newspaper reported his release for people's memories to come flooding back. That's when the college's sports director received an anonymous tip about my family tree and decided to distance the college from me, stating that it was in the best interest of their program, even though he admitted that I was one of the best PTs they'd ever hired. Even still, he felt the risk was too high just in case the information ever came out that the father of one of their employees did fifteen years for sports racketeering.

It's not as if I was the one working for the mob and bribed an elite soccer team. Still, the college didn't want to chance the possibility that it could hurt their ability to recruit high-performing high school players to their college program if players and their families saw my employment with the team as potentially hazardous to the program, thus hurting their chances at being drafted in the NFL.

I mean, people lost their homes, retirement... whatever they gambled on that game, and fans of soccer lost their trust in organized sports that day.

My uncle had one more surprise up his sleeve last week. He told me that he pulled in a favor with one of the high-ups in the organization and got me an interview for a PT opening whose job posting had already been taken down.

I applied for about thirty other PT positions within a twenty-five-mile radius after I was let go, but I received zero callbacks-even with the letter of recommendation that the college wrote for me. That's when I knew that if I wanted to do what I love, I'd need to move to a bigger city where no one knew who I was. Or, more accurately... a bigger city where no one knew who my father was.

"Here we are—Sam Roberts' office," she says, stopping in front of a large door stained the same deep espresso as the floors, with Sam Roberts, General Manager, written on a bronze plaque and drilled into the door.

She twists the doorknob and walks through. I follow as she leads me into a large waiting room with a sofa and coffee table to my left and a receptionist desk to my right and up against a back wall that seems to lead to Sam's office door.

"Cammy, this is Keely Woods," she says, tossing a thumb over her shoulder toward me as she leads me up to a receptionist's desk where a bright-eyed woman at least ten years younger than me sits with a wide smile as her eyes drift over to me. "She's a last minute addition to the interview schedule for Brenda's replacement in Sports Therapy. Sam knows about it."

Cammy stands out of her chair and leans across her desk as soon as I take the last steps up to her desk.

"Of course, welcome! I'm Sam and Penelope Roberts' assistant. Penelope mentioned you'd be coming in. It's great to meet you, Keely."

I slide my hand into hers and we shake.

"It's nice to meet you too. I almost can't believe I'm standing in the office of the GM for the Hawkeyes hockey team," I tell her.

Adel turns to me. "Cammy is the daughter of one of our players—Seven Wrenley. She's a wealth of knowledge, and she'll be the one corresponding with you for the duration of the interview process going forward."

I turn back to Cammy, unable to hide my surprise.

"Your father is Seven Wrenley, the Hawkeyes goalie?" I ask.

She nods with a proud smile across her lips.

"Your father is a legend," I tell her, but I'm sure she's already aware.

"Oh God, don't tell him that. He's hard enough to deal with as it is. The man doesn't need a bigger ego," she winks.

"Don't worry, I'll keep it to myself," I tell her.

I know she must be joking because Wrenley has been around long enough in the NHL that even I know that the man hasn't taken an interview in over a decade, and it's rumored that he refuses meet-and-greets with fans unless it's for a kid or a charity function. He keeps his head down when walking out of the Hawkeyes stadium and lets all the other players get the praise, seemingly uninterested in anything besides just playing the game he's hired for.

Adel turns her head to glance over at me. "I need to get back to my desk but I'm leaving you in good hands."

"Thank you, Adel," I tell her.

"Not a problem. Good luck and I'll see you on your way out," she says.

Then she turns and heads for the door.

Cammy opens her mouth to say something, but then the door to Sam's office opens, and a tall man with dark hair peppered around his ears stands on the other side of the door. My guess is that he's about the same age as my father—somewhere in his fifties.

He smiles the moment he sees me.

"You must be Keely Woods. My one o'clock interview?" he asks.

"Yes, sir, I am."

"Great. Come on in," he says, pulling the door open wide for me to pass through his office door. "Hold my calls, Cammy. Unless Phil Carlton calls with the new sponsor deal info. I need to know the minute that the contract comes through the legal office."

"Sure thing," I hear Cammy say as I take several steps through the threshold.

I hear the door click closed and then Sam takes steps behind me. My eyes dart around the room to take it all in.

Most of the pictures in his office are of a girl in ice skates—Penelope Roberts—with the most recent pictures of them together with the Hawkeyes center, Slade Matthews, as she sports her Olympics jacket and bouquet of roses in her hand.

I remember Penelope Roberts' huge return to the figure skating world. She and her partner took the world by storm. It was the feel-good story of the Olympics.

"Go ahead and take a seat," he says, walking around me, pointing to the two black leather chairs on the other side of his desk. "I hear that you're related to the one-and-only Oakley Humphries."

He lowers himself in his office chair, and the leather groans under his weight.

"Yes, that's right." I'm about to mention that Oakley is my father's brother but I bite my tongue before I let the words go. I'm not trying to pull a fast one over Sam's head by withholding information, but the likelihood that this interview will turn into a job offer is almost laughable. There's no point in giving away information that Sam doesn't need to be privy to. I hate the way that people in the sports world look at me when they know what my father has done. There's so much judgment and blame that gets cast my way. As if I knew anything about what my father was doing at the tender age of fourteen years old. "I just moved here from Arizona last week and I am beyond grateful for the opportunity to interview for this position. Without seeming too forward, Mr. Roberts, this is my dream job."

A job that feels more out of reach than ever before, due to who I'm related to.

"Sam, call me Sam, please," he says, pulling my paper resume off his desk to review it.

My clasped fingers, laying in my lap, begin to fidget, and I swallow down the lump in my throat as I watch Sam's gray-blue eyes dart from one side of the resume to the other.

"I see that you have a few years of experience working in a team sports environment for the University of Mesa. How did you like the work you did there? How was it working with a team of players?" he asks, still scanning my resume as he listens.

"I loved the busy days and the fact that nothing was ever the same. Working one-on-one with each player keeps every day fresh and different. Not a single player had the same needs as another. I really enjoyed the preventative work that we did there, implementing stretching and strengthening techniques during their workout routine to avoid future injury out on the field."

He nods, seemingly content with my answer.

"Why sports therapy? Once you received your masters in PT, what made you decide to put more hours into training and schooling in order to get your doctorate and sports therapy certificate?"

It's a good question, but one that I never had to ask myself when I decided to pursue Physical Therapy early on in my life.

"I have a passion for working with athletes. I played soccer in high school but tore my ACL and needed surgery. My mom took me to a DPT who specialized in sports injuries, Dr. Paula

Jacobs. She spent more time with me than our allotted appointment time and even let me come in after my insurance stopped paying. To be in a field, where you get to do that sort of good and make a difference in people's lives drew me to it. I didn't get to return to the field before I graduated but that solidified it for me. I want to help others like she helped me."

And maybe, in some ways, this feels like a way for me to give back to the sports community when my father only took from it. Like a balance sheet that I'm desperately trying to even out. It feels like a losing proposition, but I have to try.

"And the reason for the six-month gap in your resume?"

I didn't include the college's letter of recommendation. It's better that I move on from here on out. Try to make a name for myself and prove that I'm really good at my job.

So I lie.

"I waited until the end of the season and then resigned since I knew I would be moving to Seattle to spend more time with my uncle. I wanted to make sure that the college had ample time to find my replacement. Finding a good DPT who cares about the athletes and specializes in preventative care and sports injury isn't easy."

"Yes, I know," he smirks.

"Right. I'm sure you do." I let out a small snicker.

Sam Roberts has been in the sports world for longer than I've been alive. Of course he knows how difficult it is to find a PT that fits with the team. Every team's needs are different and every sports therapy program has a playbook of its own.

"Let me be upfront and honest with you, Keely. The position we're filling is to replace our very talented PT, who is leaving us permanently in a couple of months for maternity leave. The job wouldn't start right away, and though I think you have the most passion for your line of work of anyone I've interviewed so far, you also have the least amount of years of experience and haven't worked on professional athletes like all of the other candidates."

I lower my head, attempting to hide my disappointment, but I knew this would be the result.

"I understand completely, and I'm extremely grateful that you gave me a chance to interview, sir."

"Sam," he corrects again. "And I haven't made my decision yet. I have a lot to consider, and since the position isn't open for a couple of months, I have some time to determine which applicant will suit our team best."

The sound of Cammy's voice comes over the phone's intercom.

"Sorry to interrupt, but Phil Carlton just called. He said that the contract came in, and he's heading over to legal's office."

Sam hits the intercom button to respond.

"Thanks for letting me know. Keely and I just finished up. I'll head there now."

He lets go of the intercom button and then stands—I stand next, trying to appear casual as I wipe the nervous sweat from my hands against my navy slacks before our goodbye handshake.

"It really is a pleasure to meet you. Your passion for this field is evident in the way you talk about it, and whoever inevitably hires you will be lucky to have you on their team, I'm sure of it."

"Thank you," I say, warmth blooming on my cheeks.

This is the first time I've ever blushed while being rejected, but receiving a compliment like that from a legend in the hockey world means a lot to me. The sincerity in Sam's eyes leads me to believe he means every word. Even if I'm doomed never to find a job out here in Seattle, hearing those words from Sam is reason enough for me to have made the trip.

Now I need to head back to the studio apartment and prepare for tomorrow night. The Hawkeyes will be heading to my uncle's bar after the game tomorrow, and I need to work on memorizing all fifty beers and hard ciders that my uncle has on tap.

I haven't had to cram like this since college but I'm ready for a new challenge. The people on the West Coast take their beer extremely seriously. God forbid someone asks me to recommend a good IPA and I suggest a lager or an ale. They'll hand me my ass and then laugh me out of the bar.

No, that can't happen.

On the way home, I'll have to stop for my no-fail study snack—hot popcorn with M&M's poured inside. I can almost taste the melted chocolate and crunch of the popcorn already.

Then, bring on the flashcards!

Chapter Two

The Next Day

Reeve

It's the last few seconds of the game.

The scoreboard is tied, and we're in overtime.

My eyes lock onto the left wing of the opposing team. He's hauling ass straight for me with the puck in his possession.

He's leaning forward, skating full speed toward the goal, his eyes menacing and focused through his face mask.

This is the game-winning goal for them if I let this slide past my defenses—we both know it. There won't be time left on the scoreboard for retaliation by the Hawkeyes to get in a goal of our own.

I watch his eyes dart side to side, searching for my weak spot. He only needs a sliver of space to sink that three-inch puck into the net. He doesn't need much, just for me to fuck up by a mere few inches.

His defense is doing their job to keep my players off their left wing, and he gets out in front where my team won't reach him in time.

It's between me and him.

These are the moments I live for.

The moments that drive me to practice more hours on the ice than any other play on the Hawkeyes team.

The reason why I study every millimeter between goal post to goal post and practice stopping a puck in every possible pocket of open space until it's all just muscle memory.

A hockey puck can travel at speeds of over one hundred miles per hour, and with ten players out in front of me, of which five are trying to play hot potato with the puck so that I can't keep track of who has possession before they take their shot, muscle memory isn't just my best defense, it's my only defense.

I have to be able to react without even thinking.

Every one of my senses has to be acutely aware of my surroundings if I want any chance of stopping the other team from scoring.

I prepare for his assault.

Readying myself for the moment that he wields his hockey stick, taking a shot while aiming the puck in the direction that he thinks he sees a lack of coverage.

I widen my stance, my skates shifting under my weight on the ice, preparing myself to move in any direction to block the puck no matter where he decides to deposit it.

He pulls his hockey stick back and takes his shot.

Before I can even think to move, my body does it for me. I drop down to my knees stopping the puck with my pads before it can pass through between my legs.

Everyone scurries around the net, attempting to take control of the puck.

The goaltender for the other team skates further out front, almost as if he's expecting to celebrate with his team but he stops when he realizes that the puck didn't make it past me and their victory isn't secured.

He's too far off the net for comfort and I can already see him retreating—heading back for home.

The second I look down I realize that I could easily take possession. With only two seconds left on the clock and a clear shot at a defenseless goal on the other side of the rink, I make a split-second decision to do something I've only ever attempted in practice.

I take a deep breath, pull back on my hockey stick, and slap the puck as hard as I can. I can almost hear the sound of the puck whizzing through the air.

I watch in slow motion as the biscuit flies over the heads of the other players.

All ten of them immediately turn on their skates and start bolting for the other side of the rink as if their lives depend on it.

It might not be their lives, but our paychecks and our bragging rights sure as hell do.

In my peripheral, the entire stadium leaps to their feet, including all the players and coaches sitting in their respective boxes. The rink goes eerily quiet as everyone watches the puck fly over the ice, headed for its intended target.

I hear the faint sound of the opposing goaltender cursing out something like "Oh shit" as he tries to make a mad sprint for the net, which he left completely exposed.

In his defense, he couldn't have thought I would have taken that shot. It's only ever been pulled off a few times in the history of the NHL during an in-season game. It was a desperate attempt, but with two seconds left on the clock and an entire off-season of practicing the shot by myself in this exact same rink, I had to try.

The second that the puck drops onto the rink, everyone watches with bated breath as the puck slides into the net.

"SCORE!" the announcer yells over the loudspeaker, and the home crowd erupts in celebration. Meanwhile, the away team fans stare at the puck sitting against the net in disbelief.

The Hawkeyes team in the box go crazy, throwing whatever hockey gear they have in their hands up into the air. Hockey sticks and helmets fly everywhere as they jump out onto the ice and skate full force towards me, yelling at the top of their lungs, trying to compete with the cheers of the fans—but there's no chance they can yell over the sound of thousands of fans spraying beer everywhere and ripping their jerseys in full hulk mode as they lose their ever-loving minds over the goal I just made.

I glance up to see the scoreboard change from 3-3 to 4-3. The jumbotron shows my team picture with large letters overtop.

"GOAL!" it reads.

Within seconds, Lake Powers slams into me first and engulfs me in a bear hug. "What the fuck was that?" he yells, a giant smile stretched across his face.

Then Brent, Briggs, Slade, and Kaenan all join in. Soon, Seven and the rest of the team surround us, cheering and slapping me on the shoulder, back, and helmet... However, they can reach me.

We won another game.

But we still have a long way to go before the championships.

After exiting the showers, I head for the locker room.

Lake, Brent, and Seven are already pulling on slacks and buttoning up dress shirts for the press waiting for after game interviews.

"That was some impressive shit out there tonight, Reeve," Seven says.

I've looked up to Seven since before I ever made it to the NHL. He's not one to say much to anyone, let alone praise, unless it was an exceptional show of talent. But he's different ever since he started dating his new girlfriend, Brynn.

He seems happy.

"Yeah, when were you going to tell me that you could sink a puck into the net from across the rink? That would be some useful information for your captain to know," Lake teases.

"Not all of us spend our summers frolicking in Aspen with our hot girlfriends while volunteering at animal shelters. Reeve's been working on that shot on his off time," Brent jabs with a smirk.

I chuckle at Brent's comment.

Not because I found it comical, but because Brent isn't coming to my defense. He just likes to flick shit at whoever gives him the chance.

Locker room shit-talking isn't anything new. Most of the guys on the team are exhibitionists... looking for attention. It comes with the territory of playing game after game in front of large crowds of people.

After all, we're in the business of entertainment when it really comes down to it.

And being noticed doesn't hurt when it comes to jersey sales, contract negotiations, media attention and sponsorship offers.

I get it.

But I'm more of a spectator.

"I'm not apologizing for spending the summer locked up with Tessa in our Colorado house. We have a no-clothes rule the minute we walk through the front door. And have you seen that woman's ass?" he asks and then puts his fingers to his lips and gives a chef's kiss, and then sends me a wink.

"I'll have to take your word for it. As a rule of ethics, I avoid checking out any player's wives or girlfriends," I say.

"Good," Seven growls under his breath.

Yep, Brynn's a big change.

"Tessa's a workaholic. Between my away games and her work schedule, I'd never see her if I didn't ship her perfect backside off to Aspen to spend the summer with me."

"We get it. You've got a hard-on for your fiancé. Save it for the honeymoon," Brent says, throwing a towel at Lake's head.

Lake catches it just in time.

I pull my own suit out of my locker and start with boxers, then the slacks.

"Our schedules don't make relationships easy to navigate," I say, buttoning up my shirt.

This is why being single can be easier to manage, though it's lonelier when you don't have someone to call at the end of a game.

There's no one special waiting outside of the locker room for you to come out and jump your bones. No one waiting to pick you up with the team bus drops us back off in front of the stadium after away games.

Lake turns to me. "You're right, it doesn't. And though I appreciate your work ethic, probably more than most, you need something outside of hockey. Finding a partner like Tessa changed things for me."

"He's right," Seven says. "I never thought I'd say this, but you need someone to help you disengage for a couple of months before you burn out. Buying a beach house to get away for the summer wasn't enough as it turns out."

I want a wife and kids someday—the family that I never had after my parents divorced. I was too little to remember Christmas or birthdays as a family in Alaska.

It's in the long-term plan.

I'm not like Lake and Seven. Nothing in my past has sworn me off relationships, marriage or kids. For me, it's in the timing..

I've been fixated on hockey and my career to a level that some might consider unhealthy. But to be the best, you have to train like it's your life. At this point in my career, I'd make someone a terrible husband—I'd never be home.

If I thought Sam wouldn't kick me out, I'd probably set up a cot in the locker room and live, eat, and sleep hockey.

Call it an obsession, call it an addiction. Call it whatever you want as long as you call me the best that ever lived.

I want the legacy that Coach Bex, Sam Roberts, and Seven Wrenley all have.

When the day finally comes for me to retire, I want to be known as one of the best goaltenders to ever play the game.

And it's not as if I haven't dated. My last relationship ended a year ago, and we had been together for a little over eight months. She needed more attention than I could give her, so she ended things, and I was relieved. Being in a relationship while trying to focus on the playoffs was a huge distraction, which is why I'm steering clear of relationships until after I raise that Stanley Cup over my head at the end of this season.

Is it cold that I wasn't affected by our breakup? Maybe, but ever since I was young, I've only wanted one thing— to win a hockey championship.

"You ladies done checking yourselves out in the mirror yet?" Coach Bex asks, already dressed in his suit. "Media is waiting. Let's get out there. The sooner we're through with press, the sooner we can head to Oakley's. I need a drink after that overtime. That was too damn close."

Brent's completely dressed and walks up to Coach Bex, tossing an arm over Bex's shoulder.

"You're coming out with us tonight?" Brent gleams.

"If you take your arm off of me, I'll think about it," Coach Bex says.

Brent just chuckles.

Coach Bex is wound tight but for some reason, Brent thinks he's close to cracking. I'm not so sure.

I respect Bex Townsend.

We all do.

He has the most Stanley Cup wins of any player on this team. He won three championships as a player before he retired, and Phil Carlton begged him to come back and coach for him, offering him one of the highest-paying salaries for a coach in NHL history.

Before Coach Bex walks out with Brent, Bex turns to glance over his shoulder at me.

"That was a hell of a shot tonight, Aisa. You made your team proud."

It's all he says, and then he turns and heads out of the locker room's double doors.

Brent gives me a wink and a nod as if that was some confirmation that the days of Coach Bex being a hardass are numbered.

I'll believe it when I see it.

Receiving praise from both Wrenley and Townsend on the same night shows that staying focused on my career instead of my personal life is the right decision. It's where I should be.

Domestication can wait for when I can give a woman the attention she deserves.

And that night isn't tonight.

Instead, tonight, I'll celebrate with my team.

Chapter Three

Keely

My beer-flashcard-cramming-session and the M&M popcorn from last night paid off.

Oakley's fills up with Hawkeyes fans quickly tonight, even before the first puck drops.

There's nothing better than watching the home team heroes play a heated game against a rival team that pushes into overtime while packed into a local bar with white and turquoise Hawkeyes' jerseys as far as the eye can see.

The energy in this bar is so intoxicating that it reminds me why I love sports so much.

People of all different walks of life, regardless of age, gender, or political affiliation, are all pulling for one singular desire: for their favorite team to win.

I see a lady in her late seventies clinking beer glasses with a biker dude in his leathers and a jacked bodybuilder high-fiving a woman wearing gothic style attire..

And that last play by Reeve Aisa, one of the team's goalies... Well, I've never seen a group of people celebrate so hard the moment the puck slid into the net. I wouldn't be shocked in the least if the jumping up and down by the crowd of people in here cracked the foundation of this building. I swear I could feel it shudder.

The teams' interviews have been over for at least an hour, and I suspect that the players will start streaming in at any moment.

My uncle and two bartenders, Aaron and Emma work diligently behind the bar together, filling orders and taking payments as patrons belly up to the bar to put in their orders and shuffle around the bar with a tray, picking up empty bottles and glasses from tabletops while asking if they would like anything else.

I have yet to look like a stammering idiot when people ask me for a local IPA or if we have any oatmeal stout on the menu. I'm able to list off the ten different flavored hard ciders we carry and the six different brands that brew them.

It's just after eleven when I see the first couple of players walk through the doors in rain jackets and jeans, looking like they got caught in a tsunami. It's been storming all day so it's no surprise that the rain still hasn't let up. After all, it's October, and it's Seattle. Rain is to be expected.

I walk to the back of the bar and set down my tray of empty beer bottles on the counter near my uncle, who's standing by the card reader running a payment.

He stands there waiting for the receipt to print.

"You never told me how the interview went with Sam Roberts," he says.

I shrug and push the tray of empty glasses and beer bottles through a window that leads to a room with a large dishwasher. As soon as Aaron and Emma get caught up with drink orders and don't need my uncle anymore, he'll start a load in the washer and sort the bottles for recycling pick up tomorrow.

"Sam was really nice. But as I suspected when you mentioned that you got me an interview, I'm still a few years of experience away from a position at the professional team level. I appreciate that you called in a favor, though. It was thrilling just to get an interview with the Hawkeyes GM."

"Did he say you were out of the running? Or are you being too hard on yourself as usual?" he asks with one graying, bushy eyebrow downturned with skepticism.

My uncle doesn't mince words or sugarcoat anything, and I like it that way.

My father is the opposite. He always knows what you want to hear in order to lower your defenses.

"It doesn't really matter either way. The job doesn't start for another couple of months, and I need something now. I have an interview tomorrow with one of the local private school athletic directors, and that's promising. She sounded really excited over the phone about our meeting in the morning," I tell him.

The receipt for the card payment finally prints and he tucks it into a black plastic holder with a pen for the customer's signature.

"You're not in that big of a hurry to get a job, are you? You told me that you still have some money in savings, and you can stay in the studio apartment above my garage for as long as you want, Keely."

"I know," I tell him, giving him a reassuring grin. Ever since my father went to prison when I was in eighth grade, my uncle has been checking in on me and my mom frequently. It was tough for him to do a whole lot since he had Oakley's to take care of and lived hundreds of miles away, but I knew I could call him if I needed anything, and he'd show up in a heartbeat. "You've been incredibly generous, and I know that you're not trying to push me out, but the sooner I get back on my feet and start turning Seattle into my home, the better I'll feel."

He purses his lips together but he can't argue. He knows that this is a huge adjustment for me and that I feel a little bit like a fish out of water after moving away from the city I grew up in.

I was lucky to get into a college not far from home and then I got a job back in Mesa right after school. I've never lived anywhere else.

"Did you call Jaxson, the guy who runs the city league soccer team yet? He comes in every week with the Tuesday night co-ed team for drinks after their game. You could talk to him about it then. He said they have another opening. It might be a good place for you to make friends," he says as if he's my mom dropping me off on my first day at a new school.

"I haven't called him, but I will."

Though I'm still not sure if I'm ready.

My physical therapist, Dr. Jacobs cleared me to play years ago, but going back to play means that I'd have to put myself out there again, which would take me out of the bubble I have become comfortable living in.

He gives me a stern glare and then turns to hand the bill to the customer waiting for it. He already suspects what I know... that I won't be calling Jaxson, or anyone else from any city soccer league.

"Hey, can you clear that table over by the pool tables? It's starting to fill up with empty beer bottles." he says, deciding to fight the good fight another day.

I appreciate his professionalism in not handling family squabbles during working hours.

I follow his line of sight to find a table full to the brim with empty beer bottles and glasses. It seems to be the discarded drink dumping spot for all of the patrons standing around the busy pool tables now that the Hawkeyes game is over and everyone needs a new source of entertainment.

I grab my tray and head straight for it.

I get to work right away, clearing the glasses.

A few minutes later, I hear a voice right behind me.

"You're new here, aren't you. I haven't seen you at this bar before."

I turn to find an older man with slightly graying hair, glossy chocolate brown eyes, and probably a few inches taller than my five-foot-five height.

"Yes, I am. I started last week. Are you a regular?" I ask, attempting to be polite, though his body language signals to me that I should stay alert.

"I haven't been here in a while, but I'll make a greater effort to show up more frequently if I know that you'll be here," he says, taking a step closer.

I don't feel comfortable with how close he's standing or how he leans in when he talks. Nor do I like the fact that his eyes are glued to the small amount of cleavage that's noticeable from the top of my V-neck shirt.

"I'm Charlie," he says, offering out his hand for me to take.

Before I can refuse his handshake by quickly filling them with empty beer bottles, a voice pipes up.

"Charlie, leave her alone."

I look up to find Reeve Aisa, walking up behind Charlie. I hadn't seen him walk in with the last group of Hawkeyes players. Either he slipped in without me noticing or he just got here. "And didn't Oakley ban you from this bar a while ago?"

I'm not surprised in the least that my uncle told Charlie to get lost and not to come back.

"Oakley banned me?" he asks, chuckling and glancing over at me as if Reeve must be kidding. "That's a ridiculous rumor. Where did you hear that?"

Reeve doesn't seem the least bit amused, and neither am I, for that matter. I'm just relieved that a large hockey player entered this awkward conversation and seems to not like Charlie any more than I do.

"I'd suggest that you exit this bar before Slade sees you. He's still pissed about how you harassed Penelope on her birthday last year. He didn't get to finish what you two started, but I bet he'll like to. He's still wound up from all the time he spent in the penalty box tonight so I wouldn't push your luck."

Charlie turns around with his hands up in the air.

"I didn't do anything. What... is it a crime to talk to a pretty girl now?" Charlie asks.

I don't take that as a compliment, not from him.

"Yes, when the pretty girl is doing her job and feels obligated to be nice to your creepy ass so she doesn't lose her job."

Reeve finally makes eye contact with me for a second, his full lips pulling into a lopsided grin when our eyes meet for the first time, as if to assure me that he's here to help. His eyes are a warm amber with gold flecks and I bet if I was standing really close, there would be a little bit of green in them too. His eyes are set off by his olive skin tone and thick jet-black hair, which is just long enough for it to feather when he runs his hands through it.

Without all that goalie gear covering virtually every inch of the man, it's easy to see now that Reeve Aisa is an attractive man. The large cheering section, made up mostly of women in his jersey, that the cameraman panned over to after his impossible goal tonight makes even more sense.

"Charlie!" I hear my uncle's voice over the bar.

He must have just spotted us at the table.

Better late than never.

Charlie cowers just slightly at my uncle's booming voice and then searches for my uncle's location.

My uncle is a big man. Six foot two and two hundred and fifty pounds, but I watched the man chase an unwanted customer out of the bar for trying to start a fight in some weird love triangle altercation last week. He's faster and stronger than you'd think. My uncle played running back for his varsity high school team about thirty years ago and his team went on to win four state championships.

Turns out, he's still got it.

And by the looks of it, Charlie has had first-hand experience with pissing off my uncle in the past and getting chased out of the bar... or worse, and he doesn't seem interested in a repeat.

"Fine, I'm leaving. Jesus, can't a guy get a beer or two and make a friend without being harassed?"

"No, he can't," Reeve says. "Not at this bar and not with that girl."

There's a demanding presence about Reeve. I can see in Charlie's eyes that even though Reeve seems laid back and calm with his hands still in his pockets, he knows better than to push his luck with the goalie.

Charlie then sets his eyes back on me as if I'll refute Reeve's claim. Not in this lifetime.

"Sorry Charlie," I say and shrug.

Spoiler alert: I'm not sorry at all.

"Get the hell out of my bar, Charlie," my uncle yells across the room.

Charlie eyes the bar again and then so do I.

My uncle has both of his hands flat on the bar, leaning over it with his sights locked on Charlie as if at any moment he's ready to catapult over the bar top and head straight for the unwelcome customer.

We're now starting to attract more attention, attention that I've become very accustomed to hiding from. Flying under the radar has been my goal since my father went to prison.

"Bye, Charlie," Reeve says, still as cool and calm as ever, not even a warning eyebrow.

Charlie snarls at Reeve and then spins around and heads for the front door. That's when I notice every Hawkeyes player casually rubbernecking to watch Charlie leave. They must have all been aware of what was going on but kept their distance and let Reeve handle it. Based on the fights they got in tonight, I have a feeling that if Charlie hadn't relented so easily, he would have had an entire hockey team to contend with.

"Thanks for doing that," I say, a little shyness in my voice.

It's a little embarrassing that he had to come to my aid, but I doubt Charlie would have left without being told by the six-foot-plus hockey player to ship himself to Timbuktu without a return to sender.

I grab the empty beer bottles that I had originally come by to clear off the table and then set them on my tray.

"It's no trouble. He needed to be told to leave before someone besides me got involved. None of the players or regulars like him. Oakley hates him most of all."

Hearing that Reeve seems to know my uncle well enough to know that, gives me a weird feeling of being the odd man out. Even though my uncle and I are related, these people seem to have a closer connection to him than I do. And that's probably true.

The Fear-Of-Missing-Out is so strong right now and it's the first time I've ever wondered if I should have moved to Seattle sooner. My uncle has created a life inside the world of professional sports that I've always wanted to be a part of and I had no idea until now.

"So, you're the diplomatic one in the group? The peacekeeper? Is that a common trait for a hockey player?" I lift my brow and purse my lips to suppress the smirk.

His lopsided grin turns into a full-fledged smile, indicating that he likes the question.

There's something almost boyish about the way his bright white smile softens his sharp jaw and almond-shaped eyes. But from the neck down, his six-foot-plus stature is anything but soft or boyish. He's full man and hard everywhere, proven by the way his Hawkeyes sweatshirt fits snug against his chest and his corded forearms bulge out from where the sleeves are pushed up his arms, stopping just shy of his elbows.

Just a little bit of tattoo ink peeks past the sleeve of his left arm.

"I promise you; my bite is worse than my bark."

I chuckle at the way he phrased that comment backward.

"I don't think that's how the saying goes."

"Yeah, I know. But I still mean it the way I said it."

My tongue slips out to lick my lower lip unconsciously at the thought of whether or not he's a biter in the bedroom or just a nibbler. Would he leave a mark?

God, I hope he'd leave a mark.

Proof that he was there.

His eyes shoot down to catch the movement of my tongue licking my lip. His eyes come back up to mine and now those tame irises from before have a fire in them that I hadn't seen until now.

"I wouldn't want you to have to bite anyone for me," I say, trying to shake the visual of his perfect teeth scraping over my sensitive body parts. I try to shake the thought but it's a hard one to kill. "I'll try to stay out of trouble from now on so you can enjoy your night."

He looks around the bar for a second, almost as if to detect any other threat to my well-being, or maybe I just imagined that.

"You shouldn't have any problems from here on out. The entire bar just saw that they'll have me to deal with if they decide to mess with you. And unlike you, they've all seen me in a bar fight."

My lungs seize up, forgetting how to expand and contract. A daily function that I'd like to think they've perfected over the last twenty-six years of my life.

"Someone would want to start a fight with you?" I ask, glazing over the fact that he just claimed to protect me against anyone inside this bar.

It's the first time a man has ever made a claim like that to me, though I'm sure my uncle would jump in without thinking twice. He's just never said it like Reeve just did.

My uncle is family, though, and Reeve is a stranger. He has no reason to protect me other than the fact that he wants to.

"No one here, most likely. It's mostly fans so I'm not anticipating an issue. But you'll tell me if anyone causes you problems?" he asks.

"Yeah, I will," I say, gripping the tray of glasses a little tighter.

Shivers race down my spine at the thought of someone wanting to shield me like that, though I'd be a fool to believe that it's possible.

Not that he can't protect me from some drunk idiot in the bar. I'm sure he can do that—but he can't shield me from the scrutiny of the media and the backlash I get when people find out who I'm related to. Even Reeve would run for the hills if he ever found out.

I might as well have leprosy when it comes to getting close to anyone looking for a long career in professional sports.

I cut eye contact to get some reprieve from the sincerity in his eyes that makes me feel a little guilty for not just confessing who I am right off the bat. My vision glides over his damp shirt that hugs every inch of his perfectly chiseled chest.

All of the other players are wearing windbreakers or jackets except for him.

"Did you forget your coat back at the stadium?" I ask, changing the subject.

"No. I don't need one."

I glance towards the front door of the bar as a customer walks in and I catch the pouring rain outside right before the door shuts behind them.

My eyes connect back to his.

"But it's cold and pouring outside."

"I'm a hockey player and I grew up in Alaska. I'm used to it being colder than this. It doesn't bother me."

"Oh right. I guess that makes sense," I say, instantly wanting to internet stalk the Hawkeyes player who made the kind of shot at tonight's game that a hockey fan might only ever witness once in their lifetime.

Was I a little turned-on seeing Aisa make that goal earlier this evening?

I'm a little embarrassed to admit it, but definitely. And now, seeing him in real life, hovering over me and making proclamations to protect me against anyone who dares to cause me any trouble, I'm curious what it would be like to be with someone with that much *precision*.

But that will never happen because I already like him too much to ruin his career by his direct association with me.

As he's opening his mouth to say something, Seven Wrenley walks up behind him and slaps him on the shoulder.

"We're up next. Are you ready to play?"

Seven's attention shifts to me and he takes a step forward, reaching out a hand towards me. "Hey, I'm Seven. You're Oakley's niece from Arizona, right?" he asks.

Reeve's eyes flash over to me, a little wider than before. He's surprised by the news; there's no doubt about that.

I nod and smile at Seven.

"Yeah, that's me. Keely," I tell him, reaching out and shaking his hand.

"You're the niece that just moved here?" Reeve asks.

My uncle must have told more than just Penelope that I was moving to town.

"That's correct."

"So, you'll be around for a while then?"

"I hope so," I tell him.

Reeve just stares back at me, as if he's having a conversation in his head and forgot to say any of it out loud, so I shift my attention back to Seven.

"If you ever want to watch a game, let me know. I can give you one of my season ticket seats next to my girlfriend Brynn and my daughter Cammy. I've offered the seats to Oakley before, but he's never taken me up on it since our game nights are his busiest."

That makes sense. There's no way my uncle could get away during a game

I'd love to get to see a home game in the stadium. And getting to watch from a player's seats would be amazing. How often does an offer like that come up?

"My schedule is up in the air right now since I'm helping out at the bar for my room and board until I land a job. If my uncle doesn't need me during one of the Hawkeyes home games, I'll take you up on that."

"I hope you do," he says and then turns back to Reeve. "Are you ready to kick some ass? Brent and Kaenan up against us next."

"Yeah, I'm ready. Let's go," Reeve says, but his eyes stay fixed on mine.

Seven turns and walks back towards the pool table, where a few Hawkeyes players are standing with pool sticks in one hand and beers in the other. None of them are paying us any attention, as Briggs Conley seems to be telling some elaborate story.

"It's Keely... right?" Reeve asks.

"Yeah, that's right."

"I guess if you moved here, that means I'll be seeing you around?" he asks.

"Yeah, I'll be around."

"Good," he nods. "Then you should take Seven up on his offer for the seats. Or I could always give you mine."

He searches my eyes for a moment and I'm not exactly sure how to respond back because I'm not sure if he's flirting or just being nice.

"Doesn't your girlfriend want your seats?" I ask, fishing for the answer to my question.

He smirks, and my question doesn't go unnoticed. He knows why I asked.

"If you want to know if I have a girlfriend, you could have just asked. No need to beat around the bush."

His smile widens—he's teasing.

Even half a lifetime of trying to remain invisible and blend in for self-preservation isn't enough to kill my natural competitive nature. The part of me that thrives best when playing organized sports like soccer and led me to finish first at the top of my graduating class, has me ready to counter his comment with my own observation.

"Then why offer up your seats if I was already offered a place to sit? Is it because you want to see me sitting in your seats?" I ask, giving him the same smirk he gave me.

I shouldn't be flirting back.

Nothing can come of this little banter back and forth because little does he know that being associated with me is dangerous for his career.

"Maybe I'm jealous of the idea of you sitting in another man's seat. Would it be so bad if I want to see you in mine?"

I'm taken by surprise by his claim of being jealous. So much so that I'm tongue-tied and I'm not sure how to respond.

Egging him on when I know that dating me could result in him losing his hockey career would be reckless on my part.

When I don't answer right away, he flashes me another smile.

"Think about it. I'll keep my seats open," he says, and then turns and heads for the pool table and the group of guys waiting for him.

Oh, trust me... it's the only thing I'll be thinking about for some time.

After an hour of trying to keep myself from getting caught making googly eyes at Reeve all night, my uncle walks up to me as I restock beer bottles in the under-counter fridges.

"It's getting late and you have that interview tomorrow morning. Clock out and head home, okay? You should be well rested for tomorrow's interview."

"You're sure you don't need me?" I ask, glancing around the packed bar and the two other bartenders that are still running to keep up with the demand.

It's just past eleven p.m., and since Oakley's is only open until one a.m., they only have two more hours left anyway. He's right; I do need sleep since my interview is at nine a.m. tomorrow, but I won't leave him if he needs me.

"I'm sure," he looks up and over at the crowded bar.

"Hey, Reeve!" he yells.

I fight the instant urge to duck behind the bar and hide from the eyes that turn toward my uncle's booming voice. My uncle and my father are both so similar in that way. Neither have ever minded being the center of attention, but I'd prefer to stay behind the scenes... invisible if possible. If I stay under the radar, people won't ask "Oh... aren't you that horrible mobster racketeering guy's daughter?".

Instead, I stand there, squirming in place with my eyes focused on Reeve and not at the other eyes on me.

He still has a pool stick in his hand even though he's not playing this game. He and Seven won their first few games, and based on the large chalkboard hanging against the wall behind him, they're at the top of the player bracket. They'll play the winner of this game for bragging rights and their bar tab paid for. For Reeve, it isn't much since he's only on his second beer of the night.

He turns his head at my uncle, calling out his name.

"What's up?" Reeve asks.

"Can you walk Keely out to her car? She's clocking out and it's too dark out there for her to be out alone."

The horror must be obvious on my face because Reeve's eyes shift to mine.

"No, I'm fine. I can walk by myself. I parked right across the street, so I'm not even that far away," I say, trying to reason my way out of having to be escorted out to my car by a man I shouldn't already be crushing on.

Besides, I've lived independently for so many years now. I can't even remember the last time someone walked me to my car. My dad was in prison for half of my life and my last relationship ended years ago.

"Yeah, I'm on my way," Reeve says, turning to set his pool stick in the holder against the wall and his beer down on a communal table that a few of the players are using.

My uncle turns to me. "Don't be ridiculous. We usually walk out together at the end of the night, but since the bar is busy, I can't walk out with you. Reeve isn't doing anything while he waits for his next game, and you can trust him; he's probably the only unattached player who won't hit on you."

Yeah, but he might offer me his season tickets so that he doesn't have to deal with the jealousy of seeing me in another player's seat. What would you call that?

My uncle's opinion on Reeve not coming on to me should set my mind at ease, especially since I've dated a professional player in the past, and it didn't end well.

Maybe the light banter from earlier was all that transpired between us—just talk.

"He won't hit on me? Why do you say that?"

"Because I haven't seen him leave the bar with a woman in about a year since he ended his last relationship."

He hasn't dated since his last relationship?

Did she crush him that hard?

Is he still pining over her?

"Really? Why?"

"I'm not sure."

Not that it matters if he still holds a flame for his previous girlfriend.

Reeve Aisa and the entire Hawkeyes team, for that matter, are all off-limits... for their own good. And maybe for mine too. Dating a pro athlete puts you in the spotlight. A spotlight that I'm trying to avoid.

I'm not the one who decided to work for the mob, but it turns out that I'll have to pay for those sins for the rest of my life.

Reeve starts heading straight for us. His eyes locked on mine.

"Are you ready?" he asks on the other side of the bar.

"Don't you have a pool game coming up? I wouldn't want you to miss it to walk me out. My car really isn't that far anyway. My uncle is being overprotective."

"Yeah, there's one last game. We play the winners, but Lake said he'll fill in for me until I return. And your uncle isn't overprotective. It's late out, and the visibility from all the rain isn't good tonight. You shouldn't be out alone. I'll be back as soon as you're safe in your car and headed home."

I flash a look at my uncle who makes a shooing motion toward me that means it's time for me to go.

"Fine, I'll go," I say.

But my uncle has already turned to the bar and is taking an order from a customer.

"Give me a second to grab my purse and my jacket." I tell Reeve.

I turn around to open an under cabinet door behind me and pull out my things, including a thin jacket that I brought in an attempt to stay dry. However, the jacket which is used for Arizona's fall season, is no match for the weather here.

I step out behind the bar while Reeve waits for me to walk out in front of him.

He was either taught to have manners growing up, or he wants to check out my ass as we head for the door.

Since it's him, I'm okay with either.

Chapter Four

Reeve

The minute I stepped through Oakley's tonight, my attention caught on the woman with dark auburn hair standing next to Oakley behind the bar.

I did my part to scare Charlie away but I can't do anything about the other guys in the bar who have their eyes on her.

I don't remember the last time a woman caught my interest like this. The kind of attention that makes it physically hard to look away.

Something tells me that Keely is exactly the kind of distraction that could derail my plans for a winning championship season.

Still, I couldn't pass up the opportunity when Oakley asked me to walk Keely to her car.

I follow closely behind her as we head for the door.

"You're from Arizona, right? What brings you to Seattle besides crusty ol' Oakley?" I ask, watching her ponytail swish in the dimly lit bar.

Deep shades of auburn highlights catch in the lighting.

"Crusty ol' Oakley?" she asks, flashing a look over her shoulder with a downturned eyebrow and a lopsided grin.

A fan in a Tomlin jersey is headed in the opposite direction from us with a beer in his hand not paying attention to the fact that he's about to bump into her. Her attention is on me and she hasn't seen him.. Grabbing her shoulders, I steer her around him just in time.

I take her by surprise as she quickly looks back in front of us to see that she narrowly missed the inebriated bar patron whose attention was on the table full of his friends instead of the gorgeous redhead he just about ran into.

"Whoa, thanks for that," she says, but doesn't glance back this time as she keeps walking. This time she's a little more aware of our surroundings. "So I'm guessing there's a story behind how Crusty Ol' Oakley got his name."

"There is," I tell her, though it's not technically my story since I wasn't here when it all started. "When the guys first started coming to Oakley's years ago, before even I had joined the team, Oakley was a little crotchety with the players showing up after the game and packing his small sports bar with a rowdy crowd of Hawkeyes fans. He's warmed up since and I promise, his nickname is a term of endearment. We love the guy—he treats us all like family."

I can't see her face, but her ponytail nods as we get closer to the front door.

"Now I want to hear about you. Why Seattle?"

We make it to the door and she stops and faces me, pulling her jacket from under her arm to put it on before we head out into the rain.

"Here, let me help you with your jacket," I say, hoping to buy us more time for her to give me some backstory on what she's doing here.

"That would be great, thanks," she says, handing me the thin cotton sweater material.

It's not like the waterproof windbreakers that most people in the bar all brought with them to keep dry tonight.

I pull it open for her while she slips one hand at a time through the arm holes. I lift the jacket up over her shoulders and then I release the material, letting her take it from there as she begins to zip it up.

"I moved out here to spend more time with my uncle. And I've been looking for a job as a sports Physical Therapist."

"You're a doctor?" I ask, my voice a little higher pitched than I intended.

She smiles, "Are you surprised?"

I hate to admit that I am.

Not because she's a woman. There are a lot of female PTs, and I've had a number of them work with me on my sports injuries over the years. It's just that Keely looks too young to have gone to school for long enough to be a PT. She doesn't seem older than twenty-three to twenty-four, but I guess she could be close to her thirties.

The older I get, the worse I am at guessing ages, it seems.

"No... not exactly, I just..."

Before I can finish my thought, a small group pushes through the bar's entrance, allowing for a gust of cold, wet air to swirl past us. A shiver races through Keely's body.

"Are you going to be warm enough? I can find a bigger coat for you if you need it. You're going to end up waterlogged by the time we make it to the car wearing this," I say, about ready to snag a windbreaker off any one of my teammates for her.

I'd give her mine, but it's just a hoodie that I had stuffed in my locker, which I changed into after we finished with the media.

None of the players on the team want to hit the bar in a suit and tie, so we all bring a change of clothes to go out after. I must have left my jacket back at my apartment earlier today.

My hoodie isn't waterproof either, though it's thicker than her jacket, and it would at least provide her with another layer to keep her warm. The only drawback is that I can't remember the last time I washed it.

A week ago?

Two weeks ago?

I'm not completely sure.

The best case: It smells like my deodorant and a mild tinge of sweat.

The worst case: It smells like month-old used gym socks left in a gym bag for far too long.

She glances down at her jacket and then back to me. Her green eyes are the color of jade and framed by thick black lashes;

they sparkle up at me. It's the first time I notice the light dusting of freckles over the bridge of her nose.

"Oh...No," she says, waving her hand up to dislodge any concerns that she needs more layers. "I'm fine. It's not that far of a walk to my car. I found a spot right across the street. Besides, if I'm going to be living in Seattle, I'd better get used to the rain."

She's got a point.

If it's not raining, then it's at least misting in Seattle for more days of the year than not.

The door opens again as someone walks out of the loud crowded bar with their cell phone up to their ear to take a call. Another gust of wind hits us and she shivers again.

I knew she wasn't telling the truth about the jacket being warm enough. I yank my hoodie up over my head, my t-shirt pulling up with it. I pull it down to make sure it doesn't come off with my hoodie, but I notice that Keely's eyes drop to my bare torso—her eyes widening quickly in surprise.

I smile to myself.

The interest goes both ways. I wasn't sure until now.

Instead of asking for a second time if she wants another layer, only to be shot down again, I pull my hoodie down over Keely's head.

"What are you doing?" I hear her muffled voice against the fabric of my sweatshirt until her head pokes through the top. More flyaways around her hair pull out from her ponytail and frizz around her face and I've never seen anyone look as cute as she does in my hoodie. "You're going to catch a cold out there in just a t-shirt, and then how will you play in tomorrow's game?"

She's worried about me.

I can't stop a small smile from pulling at my lips.

"Don't worry about me. I could play on my deathbed. You, on the other hand... I need you not to get sick so that you can interview well tomorrow, doc."

She chuckles. "Doc, huh? Are you planning on making that nickname a habit?" she asks.

I help her hands find the armholes, and now she looks as if my sweatshirt swallowed her.

"Oh, it's warm," she says, crossing her arms around herself, like she is hugging it.

I knew she was cold.

"A habit would suggest that I call you Doc more than once. Does that mean I'm going to get to see you again?"

I reach out for the bar door and pull it open for her to exit first.

Her eyes don't meet mine as she walks past me. Instead, her attention locks onto the outside world that I just opened the door to as she takes steps through the bar's exit.

We both step out into the midnight air and onto the cement sidewalk.

It's still sprinkling outside but it's not coming down as hard as before. My t-shirt will be damp when I return to the bar and take back over for Lake, but I won't be soaked. It wouldn't matter to me either way.

I grew up in Alaska and I play Hockey for a living. The cold and the wet don't bother me.

"Did I say something wrong? I didn't mean to pressure you into seeing me again, I just—"

Her eyes flash back up to mine as we walk down the sidewalk heading for the crosswalk, and she shakes her head. "No, you didn't say anything wrong. I would like to see you again too. It's just that..." she trails for a second. "Right now, I'm trying to focus on this new move and getting myself established in Seattle. It's just a little too soon for me to get involved with anyone."

I'm in the same situation—It's too soon for me too.

In seven months, the season will be over, and if the team works its ass off, we should have a Stanley Cup to show for it. If she plans on living here permanently, I'll get my chance later. There's no reason to rush into anything.

"You don't have to explain yourself. It's not a big deal. You're busy, and the season is in full swing for me. I wasn't trying to push anything on you."

"I know that you weren't. I just have a lot I'm dealing with right now."

I promised myself that I wouldn't get into a relationship until after this season was over and I have a championship win.

I should be happy that my moment of weakness is met with Keely's lack of availability at this time in her life.

I should be relieved, but I'm not.

I'm disappointed, but I won't let her see that.

"Have you had any luck with job interviews?" I ask.

"Not yet but I have an interview tomorrow that's promising. It's not exactly where I want to be but it's a start. I'd be working with middle school athletes at an all-girls private school, which would be cool since I was about that age when I found my love of physical therapy after my soccer injury."

"You used to play soccer?"

I like finding out all these little pieces of information about Keely.

"Yes, before I tore my ACL."

"I'm sorry to hear about your injury—that sucks. Have you been able to play since?" I ask.

"No, I haven't. But my uncle thinks I should join a city league soccer team to make friends."

"The man gives good advice. The city leagues around here take it pretty seriously. There are a bunch of good teams," I tell her. "You said that working at the all-girls school isn't where you want to be. If you could do anything, what would you do?"

Her lips purse, and her shoulders shrug, as if she's too shy to tell me. But then her lips part, and she speaks.

"My dream is to be a PT for a professional team. I don't care which sport, I just want to be a part of something big even if I only get to watch from the basement," she says, digging her hands deeper into the front pocket of my hoodie.

Watch from the basement?

Who would hide someone like Keely away?

We finally make it to the crosswalk and wait until the walk sign turns green. It's late and dark out, and the whiteness of the asphalt makes visibility poor.

The WALK pedestrian sign illuminates and we step off the curb.

I glance both ways to make sure no cars are coming even though we have the right of way. The road is eerily quiet for a busy Thursday night due to the Hawkeyes home game but the monsoon from earlier may have kept some people from coming out.

As we cross, I can't help but glance over at Keely. The yellow Street lamp illuminates her face, and the rain gives everything around us a dream-like blurred effect.

Without warning, headlights bounce across the wet asphalt, and the sound of screeching tires and a roaring engine fills my ears. Without thinking, I react—shoving Keely as hard as I can—no time to give her warning.

I hear her make a sound the moment she hits the asphalt further out of the way with an "oof" sound just before impact when the car hits my side and I'm thrown up on the hood of a vehicle I barely saw coming.

And then I feel it--the sharp pain explodes through my entire body and then I slide off the car, hitting my head on the asphalt as it brakes to a dead stop.

The last thing I hear before passing out is the screeching tires of the car as it accelerates away from me--and Keely's voice screaming for help.

"Someone called 911. He's hurt! He's hurt!"

Chapter Five

Keely

It only takes seconds for your entire world to be flipped upside down.

Sitting in the waiting room, staring vacantly down at the colorful swirls of the hospital's carpet, I wait impatiently for someone to come out and update me on Reeve's prognosis.

I don't think I'll ever forget the sound of the tires screeching on the wet asphalt, the wail of the sirens in the distance as they head for us, the crunch of the metal and glass under my feet as I ran to Reeve, my blood-soaked knees from where Reeve pushed me and I skinned them.

I barely remember the ride in the ambulance to the hospital, holding Reeve's hand, trying to talk to him to keep him awake while the paramedics checked him out for all possible injuries.

I'm sure he suffered a concussion based on what he said the moment that I got to him waiting on the asphalt face up.

"Am I dead? Is this heaven?"

"No, Reeve, this isn't heaven. You're still in Seattle."

"Then go back and tell God that he made a mistake. You're too pretty to be my guardian angel. I don't deserve you."

"I'm not a guardian angel, Reeve. It's me, Keely."

"Doc?..."

"Yeah Reeve, it's me."

"Tell my mom I'm sorry. I'm so sorry."

I was just about to ask him why he wanted me to tell his mom he was sorry when I heard the loud shouting and running of people headed straight for us. Within seconds, Coach Bex was kneeling down next to me on my right and Seven to my left, with more than half the rest of the team circling us.

With a possible neck injury, none of us touched him, but we kept him awake until the ambulance came.

Now, sitting in the waiting room with Coach Bex leaning up against a vending machine, stirring his coffee with a thin straw as he stares off into space, lost in thought, and Sam Roberts deep in the back corner of the room on a call with the owner of the Hawkeyes, Phil Carlton. I can only hear whispered tones from their conversation, but what I can make out is Sam agreeing that Reeve has to get the best care available.

It didn't take long after Reeve and I arrived in the ambulance for dozens of Hawkeyes players to show up wanting an update on Reeve, but I didn't have any. The moment we got here, they raced him off for x-rays, CT scans, ultrasounds... anything and everything they could.

Since Reeve hadn't been admitted into a room yet, I was ushered to a waiting room where I found Coach Bex pacing the floor, fielding calls while Sam discussed who the surgeon operating on Reeve would be.

My heart sank at the idea of him needing surgery but I knew that he would need it based on the condition of his leg on our way to the hospital. Guilt filled me at the idea that Reeve protected me by pushing me out of the way, but there's nothing I could do to protect him from any of this.

It's been a couple of hours since Sam and Coach Bex advised all of Reeve's teammates to go home and get some rest for tomorrow night's game. They promised that they would keep everyone posted about Reeve's condition.

My brain is just now starting to process the stinging pain of my scraped-up knees from where I fell to the rough road. Sam asked me if I wanted a nurse to look at them after we were notified that Reeve was in surgery. I had forgotten all about my knees until he mentioned it.

When I declined, he told me that I was free to leave if I wanted and he would keep me updated, but when I told him I wanted to stay, he nodded and didn't ask again.

In my peripheral vision, I see a doctor in his navy-blue scrubs and surgeon's cap walking down the hall toward the waiting room.

The moment I jump to my feet, the movement catches Coach Bex and Sam's attention, and the two men head straight for the doctor, who has a clipboard dangling at his side and his eyes fixed on me--front and center of his vision.

We all practically lunge toward him, cutting the space between us, all of us anxious to hear Reeve's prognosis.

"Dr. Morgan. How did it go?" Sam asks, the three of us standing in a semi-circle around the doctor--me being the shortest by a long shot.

The Doctor turns his attention to Sam. The moment I hear him speak, I realize that he's younger than I thought he'd be because of the high accolades that I heard Sam tell Phil Carlton over the phone.

"We got lucky. I called all the specialists we know, and they all said the same thing, that Dr. Jaxson Morgan is one of the best sports injury surgeons on the entire West Coast, and he just so happens to be on-call at this hospital."

With so many other well-known doctors already knowing about a surgeon in Seattle, I figured he must be an older surgeon with a whole lifetime of experience.

"He did well in surgery. The tear to his meniscus was worse than I thought once I got in there. However, the operation was textbook. He's going to require extensive physical therapy if he wants a chance at play at the level he used to."

"Will he be able to play this season?" Bex asks, an eyebrow raised and his lips tight.

"That will be up to Reeve and how quickly he heals. My recommendation is to get a one-on-one physical therapist as soon as possible to work with him," Dr. Morgan says.

"But do you think if someone puts the time in with him, he still has a shot at getting back on the ice before the playoffs?" I jump in with my question.

I know what it's like to lose your chance at playing the sport you love. And to potentially lose out on playing for an entire season once you hit the big leagues… Well, I just can't imagine Reeve will take it well. I worked with a college player last year with this exact injury before I was let go. He screwed up his knee in a boating accident over the summer of his senior year but the hours he and I put in getting him back out on the field paid off. He just got signed to the NFL as a first-round pick. I know if given the chance, I could help Reeve.

Dr. Morgan's dark blue eyes settle on mine.

"This is Keely Woods. She was the one who was with Reeve when he got hit by the car. She witnessed the entire thing and rode with him to the hospital in the ambulance." Sam tells him.

"Your name is Keely?" he asks me.

I nod. "Yeah, that's right. Keely Woods."

It's the first time that I notice the dimple on the doctor's right cheek when his lips pull up into a soft smile.

"They told me that someone was with him when he got hit. Any chance you remember the license plate on the hit-and-run vehicle?" He asks but there's an almost familiarity in his eyes and a softness in his tone, unlike the down-to-business surgeon he was a minute ago when he came out to offer up the news about Reeve.

One of the police investigators has already shown up at the hospital to ask me all of his questions but I didn't have much to tell him.

"No," I say, wishing I had something to offer up. "I barely saw anything. Reeve pushed me out of the way and I fell to the ground. By the time I realized what was going on and looked back, the car had already sped away and Reeve was on the ground," I say, swallowing hard at the memory of not knowing if Reeve was going to be okay.

"Oakley's has video surveillance outside. It happened a couple of blocks away, but the car drove past the bar while fleeing the scene. Oakley Humphries' is turning the video surveillance over to the investigator for the case. We'll get them," Bex says, his jaw clenching.

My uncle called me to find out if he should come to the hospital to be with me but I told him to do what he could at the bar and that I would meet him back at the house once Reeve was out of surgery. He agreed.

"Did you sustain those injuries from the accident?" Dr. Morgan asks, pointing at something.

I look down to see the dried blood and ripped denim of my jeans where my knees hit the pavement.

"Yes... I mean, I'm fine. It's nothing like Reeve's injury," I say, waving him off.

"I can ask a nurse to clean you up if you--" Dr. Morgan starts.

"No! Thank you but no... There are people here who need more help than I do. I'll take care of it when I get home, but thank you."

I break eye contact with Dr. Morgan when it seems like he would like to go against my wishes and page a nurse over. When I look over at Sam, he seems to see that I'm hoping for a conversation change and he chimes in.

"When can we see Reeve?" Sam asks.

Sam's kept a cool and calm demeanor this entire time but now I can see that it's starting to shake a little. He wasn't there at the accident with Reeve like Bex and I were, and he barely got here before Reeve was wheeled into surgery. He's anxious to see Reeve and I can't blame him.o am I.

"He's in post-op recovery right now but as soon as he's awake and ready to take visitors, I'll have a nurse bring you back to see him."

"When can he go home?" Coach Bex asks.

"Due to his injury and the concussion, they'll want to keep him today and overnight for observation, but there are no active concerns."

I wish he were going to get to go today, but I can feel the relief felt between us, three, standing side by side.

He's going to be okay, and he will get home soon.

"If there aren't any more questions, I have another patient I need to check in on," Dr. Morgan says.

"No, that's it. Thank you for all you've done," Sam says.

"We appreciate it," Coach Bex says.

Sam and Bex both reach out, shaking the doctor's hand and then Dr. Morgan's eyes shift to me.

"It was a pleasure to meet you, Keely," he says, that look of familiarity in them again, like somehow, he knows me... or of me. Maybe we met in college? But he doesn't look familiar to me at all, and I'm sure I wouldn't forget a tall, handsome pre-med student. Plus, he must have graduated years before me for him to have the position he does at the hospital.

"Please excuse me for asking.., but have we met outside of this hospital before?" I feel a little silly for asking in front of Sam and Coach Bex but it will bug me for weeks, possibly even years if I don't ask where he knows me from.

"Not yet, but we will soon. See you around, Keely."

He gives me a playful smirk before turning around and heading back down the hallway in which he came.

"Not yet but we will..."

What?

Bex turns to Sam, with me standing in the middle before Dr. Morgan is even out of earshot.

"He needs a PT before he even gets home," he tells Sam.

"I agree. Phil says that we have access to whatever funds we need to get Reeve back up and playing. We can pay for the best," Sam says.

Bex's hands pinch at his hips. "We need someone who will work with him daily and get him back on the ice."

Then Sam's eyes turn toward me. "Keely, do you still want the job with the Hawkeyes?"

"Yes, absolutely I do," I tell him, wide-eyed at his question.

"It's obvious you care about Reeve since you're still here. And right now, he could use your skills. How do you feel about being his PT and working with Reeve to get him back in shape? If you can get him back into shape well enough to get cleared for practice before the job opening for the PT position with the Hawkeyes', then the position is yours."

I can barely believe what I'm hearing.

Not only is he giving me the chance to work with Reeve, but he's also offering me a job if I can pull this off and get Reeve healthy enough to practice with the team.

I want this.

I want to show Sam that I'm ready for the position as a PT, and I owe this to Reeve.

If he hadn't pushed me out of the way, it might have been me in post-op instead of him.

"I'll do it. When do I start?" I ask.

"Right now."

Chapter Six

Reeve

My mouth tastes like cotton, and I still feel the groggy effects after waking up from surgery.

I stare down at the gray hospital-issued blanket lying over my legs as the blood pressure cuff tightens around my bicep and beeps as it takes its reading.

"Good, 113 over 68... you're perfect," the nurse standing next to me says.

She pulls the Velcro apart on the blood pressure cuff and then turns to input the information into the computer system next to my bed. "How are you feeling? Are you comfortable? I see in your chart that you don't want any pain medication."

She glances up at her. "That's correct. I don't need it. Pain meds mess with my performance."

Nurse Dolly snickers at my comment, and I realize that she took it a little differently than I meant it, unsure how to respond.

"Your performance huh? Well, listen there, young man. I'm always open to watching a good performance, especially from any of the members of the Hawkeyes team, but keep in clean, will you?" she winks, and I let out a chuckle.

"Get your head out of the gutter, Dolly; that's not the kind of "performance" I was referring to and you know it," I tease back.

"Just as well," she says, then leans closer with a playful smirk. "I'm partial to the old players anyway. No offense. Feel free to drop Wrenley or Coach Bex in my hospital bed any day."

Dolly's a feisty one and I'm grateful for the distraction as the weight of my injury is a little more than I care to handle right now.

"Gotta kick a man when he's down, do you?" I tell her.

That earns me another sly smile from my nurse.

"You won't be down for long, Hun. You'll be back up making highlight reel trick shots like you did last night. But I'd clear your "performing arts" with the doctor before you mess up that pretty knee of yours."

"I will. And when I'm back on the ice, maybe you can come watch me perform something a little cleaner."

"Oh don't bother saving me a seat. With a pretty face like yours I'm sure you have a girl clawing to get in your season ticket seats."

"Actually... I do have a girl you can sit with," I say, thinking about Keely and the last moment I saw her.

She was running after the gurney into the ER, her ponytail swishing back and forth to keep up with the EMTs and ER doctor.

"You're going to be okay, Reeve. I promise."

And then another nurse stopped her as they wheeled me past double doors that she could pass through with me. But at least she was safe. And that is worth whatever recovery I have ahead of me now.

"Oh yeah? Is it the pretty girl who came in with you in the ambulance?" she asks.

Has she seen her?

Has she been here and they turned her away.

"That's the one. Keely. Have you seen her? Is she okay?" I ask.

"As far as I know, she barely has a scratch on her thanks to you. I haven't seen her myself yet, but I know she's been here all night waiting for you to get out of surgery," I give her a lifted eyebrow, wondering how she knows all of this if she hasn't seen her. "The nurses talk. It's been a slow evening on this floor and we get restless. You can't blame us when we hear rumblings about a professional hockey player saving someone from a speeding vehicle," she says, clicking around on her mouse still, inputting more stuff into my chart. "It's swoon-worthy what you did tonight. If all the young nurses didn't already have crushes on you, they sure as hell do now."

I laugh and shake my head, dismissing her claim.

There's only one woman in this hospital that I hope has a crush on me like I have one on her, even though our timing is shit. But she stayed. She's still here.

"They'll get bored and move on... especially if I can't play anymore," I say, the gravity of that possibility a little more than I can handle.

"You're lucky, you know," she continues, breaking the silence as she organizes my chart. "You're young, and your body will heal faster than you think. Doctors do the best they can but they don't have a crystal ball. Just give it time."

"Yeah, time..." I say absently, staring out the window where the beginning of sunlight is starting to filter through clouds as the sun rises, casting a golden glow across the sky.

"You'll be back to playing in no time," she assures me, though I can hear the heaviness in her voice.

She talks a good game, but she can't give me any assurance. Not more than I can give myself.

"What if I can't play at the level I used to be able to?" The words slip out before I can catch them. They linger in the air between us, heavy and unwelcome.

Dolly glances at me, her expression shifting from empathy to something deeper, a recognition perhaps. "Then you find something new and exciting. Life is full of second acts. Trust me."

The sound of knuckles tapping against my hospital room door has Dolly and I both glancing over.

I see Sam and Coach Bex walk into my room and I wait impatiently for Keely to follow behind. Luckily, I don't have to wait long before she walks through the door. Her eyes quickly scan the room until they find mine.

I let out an exhale.

Seeing her safe again has my chest filling with emotion.

Though she appeared fine when I last saw her, I wasn't in the right frame of mind to process the information as well as I can now.

"Hi," she says, almost with a timid tone.

"Hi," I say back.

I want her to run to me.

I want her to crawl up on the bed beside me and wrap herself under the blanket with me.

It's been a long fucking day, and all I want right now is to feel her breathing and be close enough to see the pink hue in her cheeks and the freckles over her nose. My heart races as I take in the sight of her still wearing my hoodie, and suddenly, it feels like everything else that mattered has diminished in importance compared to just having her here.

She looks just a little bit like mine.

Sam walks over to the left side of my bed, staying out of Dolly's way on my right, and Coach Bex is standing at the end of my bed.

"You gave us a scare there for a minute," Sam says.

My gaze shifts between Sam and Coach Bex before returning to Keely. The warmth of her presence fills the room in a way that makes everything else fade into the background.

"How are you feeling after surgery? Dr. Morgan told us that it went well," Coach Bex says.

"Like I've been run over by a car," I joke lightly but instantly regret it when the pain kicks back in and I wince.

My eyes find Keely again, and I can see that my pain hurts her too. A shimmer with unshed emotion in her eyes.

"Hey... I'm going to be okay. Just like you told me I would be," I say, offering up my hand for her to take.

She flashes a look at Sam and Bex but then heads straight for me and takes my hand.

The memory of her holding my hand while I lay on the wet black asphalt and then again, the entire ride to the hospital flash through my memory.

"I was so scared," she whispers, biting her lower lip. "When you pushed me out of the way...and then you..."

There's guilt in her eyes, but there shouldn't be.

"Keely, what happened last night wasn't your fault. I hope you know that." I interrupt gently, wanting to erase that memory from her mind as much as my own. "You're safe now. That's what matters. I'd do it a thousand times over just to keep you away from harm."

An understanding passes between us, and I can see her shoulders relax just a fraction. I roll my thumb over her hand and the warmth in her cheeks flushes deeper—a thrill rushing through me at the sight of being able to soothe her, even if it's a small amount.

"Reeve," Coach Bex speaks up, drawing my focus towards him. "We need to discuss your rehabilitation. Dr. Morgan says that we should get you working with a physical therapist as soon as possible to give us the best results in your rehabilitation."

I'm relieved that Coach Bex wants to get right to work. He's not the kind of person to give false hope. The fact that he thinks it's worth trying to get me the best care to get me back on the ice instills new confidence in me. And I believe him more than I believe anyone else.

"Okay, what's the plan?" I ask, hopeful.

Dolly moves around the room. Sam steps back and out of her way as she comes over to my left side and pulls the blanket up over my knee to check the dressing around it.

When she seems pleased with it, she lays the blanket back down gently and smiles up at me.

"I'll leave you four to chat while I go check on some other patients. I'll be back soon to check on you, okay? No impromptu performances while I'm gone. I don't want to miss anything good; it's the only perk of this job," she teases and then turns to leave.

"Thanks, Dolly," I say.

"The plan is for the Hawkeyes to bring on a full-time physical therapist to help you. You'll have daily one-on-one sessions to get you back in the best shape we can. Penelope checked and there is an open apartment down the hall from you in The Commons. We're moving her in so that she's around for your recovery."

"You're moving her in down the hall? Is that necessary?" I ask.

I feel Keely's hand go a little slack in mine. She's not holding on as tight as she was.

"We think so," Sam says, and I'm drawn back to the urgency in his tone. "And you're getting Keely."

My heart leaps at the mention of her name, and I can't help the way my gaze snaps to hers. There's a moment of silent acknowledgment, a shared understanding of what this could mean for both of us. Her freckled cheeks flush brighter, and for an instant, I forget where I am—the hospital, the accident, the looming specter of uncertainty surrounding my return to the ice.

I can see the spark of determination igniting within her. "As long as you're okay with it," she says to me. "I've worked with an athlete who had a similar injury and I know exactly how I would start your recovery. But if you want someone else--"

"No," I say, quickly. I know that I need to put all of my focus on recovering so that I can get back on the ice, but getting to work that close with Keely while I recover will make it easier to put a relationship aside until I recover, or at least I hope it makes things easier. "I trust you. But what about your interview today?"

I don't want her to give up a good job just for me.

"I left her a voicemail when you went into surgery to let her know that I wouldn't be able to make our appointment due to an emergency."

"And I'm glad she did because we poached her," Sam smiles over at Keely.

"Good, then it's settled," Coach Bex adds with a nod. "I need to get back to the stadium and update the coaching staff and players. Keely, I leave you in charge. If you can get him back to at least practicing with the team in a couple of months, hopefully, he'll be strong enough to start next season for us."

"Wait, what? Next season?"

"Yes," Sam assures, glancing at me with a hint of pride in his eyes. "We don't want you to overdo it. If you reinjure your knee, we could lose our shot at getting you back on the ice at all."

Silence washes over us as Keely takes a deep breath, seeming to weigh the pressure put on her shoulders, but she doesn't look like she intends to back out. Finally, she looks down at me, the light catching her auburn hair, her green eyes locking on mine.

"Six weeks. I only need six weeks." I tell them, something in Keely's eyes tells me that I need to make this happen.

"Are you sure about this?" she says softly.

I stare back into her eyes.

I'm sure about one thing... Keely Woods is about to change my life forever.

"Put me in, coach."

Chapter Seven

Keely

After leaving the hospital yesterday, I went straight home and got to work on brushing up on my knowledge of meniscus injuries and how best to go forward. I called my old PT, Dr. Jacobs, and she was helpful in devising a plan for his therapy.

Just as I got off the phone with Dr. Jacobs, I got a text.

> **Unknown: Hi Keely. This is Penelope Roberts. The Assistant General Manager for the Hawkeyes. The property management company confirmed your apartment is available but you won't be able to move in until they re-key it. They said they'll have some-**

> **one down there in two days to get you new keys.**

I instantly add Penelope to my phone. I have a feeling I'll need her contact information.

> **Keely: Thanks Penelope. That won't be a problem. I'll get the key whenever they have it.**

> **Penelope: Great! I'll keep you posted. Thank you for being so flexible and jumping in to help Reeve on such short notice.**

> **Keely: I owe him one.**

The next day, I spend most of it rushing around from store to store picking up everything that I think Reeve might need when he gets home.

Though my job title is PT for this position, in all reality, my responsibilities will be significantly more extensive than that.

Already today, I picked up crutches, a wheelchair, and a shower walker since Reeve won't be allowed to submerge his surgery incisions until the stitches dissolve on their own, and a few other things to make his life a little easier.

Brent Tomlin, the Hawkeyes left wing and Slade Matthews, the center, who also all live in The Commons, came by earlier to grab the wheelchair from the apartment and a pair of loose gym shorts and a t-shirt for Reeve to come home in before they left for the hospital to pick him up.

I also picked up all of his meds from the pharmacy and a few PT items that we'll be able to use during our stretches, which I'll want to start him on as soon as possible. If we want to get him back on the ice in six weeks and I want to earn that PT opening position, he and I both have our work cut out for us.

Standing in the kitchen, organizing his meds, I notice one important item is missing. There are no pain meds in the pharmacy bag. I didn't bother to go through the bottles when they handed me the bag, I just assumed it would all be there.

I pulled out the list of prescriptions on the receipt and noticed that no pain meds were listed there either.

Weird.

I'll have to call the hospital and ask them to send a new prescription to the pharmacy for me. He'll need them to get through the pain of the surgery but also the hoops I'm about to make him jump through to get him fit to skate again.

I pick up my phone to call, but then I hear the front door of the apartment open.

"We're home!" I hear a male voice call out.

The sound of a wheelchair being pushed down the short hallway into the large one-bedroom apartment echoes through the space, and then I see Brent pushing Reeve toward the living room with Slade behind them, carrying a backpack, a pillow, and a sleeping bag.

"Are those crutches?" Reeve asks, his eyes wide with interest.

I can already tell that the coloring in his cheeks is better today than it was yesterday after surgery. But post-surgery pain is the worst twenty-four to forty-eight hours after surgery so things will get worse before they get better, especially if I can't get his pain meds filled today.

"Yes, why?" I ask but he's already starting to stand out of the wheelchair on one leg, his other leg lifted enough not to touch the ground.

He groans out in pain, but his face shows he's determined.

"Whoa, whoa," Brent calls out, trying to keep the wheelchair steady.

"Where the hell do you think you're going?" Slade says, trying to get around Brent and the wheelchair before Reeve crashes to the ground.

I bolt around the kitchen island, headed straight for him. "Reeve, hold on, let me help you."

"I've had enough of being carted around in a wheelchair by this maniac. Thank God he decided on a career in the NHL and not in NASCAR. His car wouldn't make it even one lap around the track still in one piece. Plus, I'm starving. The hospital food sucks."

I pull the crutches off the couch where I leaned them up against it earlier. I part the two crutches and then hand Reeve each one, standing close by until they're tucked safely under his armpits, just in case he loses balance.

"Thanks for picking all this stuff up," he says, his amber eyes connecting with mine, a soft smile across his lips.

The height of the crutches will need to be adjusted because he's so tall, but he's already hobbling his way over toward the kitchen. He tries to hide the groans of pain each time he takes a step with the crutches, but I hear them.

"What?" Brent says, gaining our attention again and tosses his hands up. "I ran him into one gurney on the way down the hall. No one was even on it, and now he refuses to give me a 5-star review for my transportation services."

"Yeah, can you believe the nerve?" Slade teases, heading for the living room.

"You ran me into a parked truck in the parking lot," Reeve says, already scouring through the fridge for something to eat.

"Such a baby. You grazed the bumper at best." Then Brent looks over at me when he realizes that he won't get sympathy from Reeve or Slade. "Typical goalie. Such an ice princess. He doesn't know anything about being slammed against the sidewalls. If he did, he wouldn't be grumbling about a low-speed fender bender with hospital equipment."

I laugh and then I notice Slade dropping the pillow, sleeping bag and backpack on the couch in the living room.

"What's all that for? Reeve didn't have that in the hospital with him, did he?" I ask, though I know the answer based on what he had in the ambulance when we showed up.

"I'm staying the night tonight--doctor's orders. They want someone with him tonight," Slade says.

"Overkill. I'll be fine," Reeve mutters from the kitchen, with a mozzarella cheese stick in one hand and a chocolate protein shake in the other.

"Well, if someone has to stay, I'll do it. You don't need to. My apartment isn't ready yet, so I'll take your spot on the couch."

Brent and Slade both look at Reeve for his answer.

When my attention shifts to him in the kitchen, he's standing there as if he just stopped eating when I proposed the new sleeping arrangement.

"I just got hired to help during his recovery, it makes more sense. And my uncle Oakley's apartment is over fifteen minutes from here so if he needs something, I won't have to drive across town," I say, looking at all three of them since no one has answered.

Slade and Brent keep their eyes on Reeve, waiting for his answer.

"Plus, she actually knows what the fuck she's doing with the meds. Slade would end up giving you too much of something and you'd end up foaming at the mouth of having the runs for a month--some shit like that," Brent shifts his gaze to me. "Oh... sorry for the cursing."

"It's fine," I chuckle.

I'm used to the locker room talk, so cursing is the least offensive thing I've ever heard.

"I can read a prescription bottle, Brent; I'm not stupid," Slade says.

"I wouldn't be so sure. The jury's still out, and they're taking a long weekend."

Reeve and I both laugh--our eyes connecting--and then he downs the last of his protein shake.

"Are you sure you're okay with staying? I doubt you snore as loud as Slade."

"Hey! I heard that," Slade says in the living room.

"Is that the prerequisite? Whoever snores the quietest gets to stay?" I ask.

Though I wouldn't blame him. He probably didn't sleep well last night.

It's hard sleeping in a hospital with machines going off and nursing staff coming in frequently to check on vitals.

"And you'd better like the Discovery Channel."

"The Discovery Channel? Really? Why?"

"Shark week," Brent and Slade say in unison.

"Your teammates know you well."

Reeve just shrugs, opening up a cardboard pizza box that he just pulled from the fridge. I'm guessing leftovers from earlier this week. Or at least I hope so.

"Well then, if you don't need us, we'll get out of your hair and let you get settled," Brent tells me. "But if you need any help, let us know. Most of the players live in this building, except Kaenan Altman and me. But we're all available to babysit the cripple if you need to run an errand."

"Oh, speaking of," I say, reaching for my phone. "I need to call the hospital and tell them that they forgot to send your pain meds to the pharmacy."

The three of them share a look as I unlock my phone.

"You don't need to make that call, Keely," Reeve says.

I can't tell if it's my imagination or if Brent and Slade squirm at Reeve's response like they know something I don't.

"Why not? You're going to be in pain as soon as whatever they gave you in the hospital wears off," I protest.

This doesn't make sense. Why wouldn't he want the meds? He was hit by a car not even thirty-six hours ago.

"We're taking off. We'll see you guys later," Slade says, grabbing his pillow, sleeping bag, and backpack off the couch and heads for the front door.

"I'm serious about calling any of us. There's a Hawkeyes contact list magnetized on the side of the fridge. We all have one and everyone's name and number from the franchise are on there. Call day or night," Brent says.

I nod, and then Brent turns, taking one last look at Reeve.

"Looks like you're going to be in good hands tonight. Lucky bastard," Brent says with a grin and then leaves, following Slade out.

I wait until I hear the door shut on the apartment and then I ask the question.

"What's the deal with the pain meds?"

"I just don't need them. I don't like the way they make me feel different. I need to stay sharp out on the ice at all times. I don't drink during the season unless we win our game that night and I go out with the guys to celebrate. Then I stick to a two-beer minimum."

He finishes his fourth slice of pizza and then motions to the last slice as if to ask if I want it.

"No thanks, I ate before I got here."

He picks up the last slice to polish off the leftover box.

"Is there any other reason I should be aware of for why you don't want to use prescription narcotics to handle your pain? The more I know, the better I can help you."

He shakes his head, picking up the empty box and dumping it in the recycle bin. "Nope," he says simply.

"I'm going to be asking you to push through your limits in order for us to get you back out on the ice and ready to play. You're going to be in a lot of pain without some kind of pain management."

"Give me your worst Doc, I can handle it. If I couldn't, I wouldn't have survived the last twenty-five years of my life dedicated to a career in hockey."

"I'm going to remind you of the big talk you just laid down when you're on your knees begging me for mercy when we start getting to the real work."

"Keke," he says, leaning over the island and using a new nickname that I've never heard him use before. "I have no doubt in my mind that before this is all over, you'll have me on my knees...begging."

We hold each other's stare for a moment, and then I clear my throat. No matter what I want or what he wants, I have to remind myself that being his PT is the only thing that can happen between us or else it could cost him sponsorship deals or even his career.

He doesn't know it yet, and I'm too embarrassed to tell him, but getting involved with me isn't worth it.

"Come on. My knee is starting to hurt," he says. "Come sit with me and watch the Discovery channel while I ice it."

"Oh... you're actually serious about the Discovery Channel?" I ask.

"Well, yeah, only a psychopath would lie about that. But first, let's get you out of the scrubs," he says heading for his bedroom.

I follow him into his room—he pulls out one of his old high school hockey t-shirts and a pair of boxer briefs. "They might be a little big on you but they're better than the scrubs you have."

"You don't like the scrubs?" I ask.

"It makes me feel like you're an in-home care nurse, and I'm your geriatric patient. I'm all for role-play, but with the potential of retiring from hockey if I don't recover back to optimal condition, it hits a little close to home, you know?"

I just chuckle and pick up the clothes he lays on the bed.

"Good to know. I won't wear the scrubs anymore if you don't like them. How about you head for the couch and get comfortable? I'll change, and then I'll grab the ice pack."

"I think I have a brand-new gallon of Rocky Road ice cream in the freezer. Grab two spoons."

He starts working his way slowly to the couch.

For the love of God, Keely... you're so close to your dream of working for a professional team.

Whatever you do, don't fall in love with Reeve Aisa.

Chapter Eight

Reeve

Sitting here next to Keely on my couch, eating ice cream with her in my clothes, and watching the large Alaska fishing vessel show is the last thing I would have thought I'd be doing right now, but here we are.

The best part about tonight is the information dumps she gives me during the commercial breaks.

My knee is killing me right now, but I won't let Keely see the pain it's causing me. She set me up with a spot on the couch and scrounged around the house to find every pillow she could for elevating my leg. She keeps on top of making sure that I have a new ice pack from the freezer each hour to keep the pain down to a dull throbbing instead of the sharp stabbing pain it is if the ice pack gets too warm.

If she thinks I'm managing the pain well enough with ice packs, I'm hoping she'll stop asking about why I won't take anything for the pain.

Everyone has a piece of their past that they'd rather not drum up, and I'm no different.

I watch as she dips her spoon into the carton of Rocky Road ice cream that I'm holding up in my hand for her. And then I watch as her full pink lips wrap around the spoon to take her bite.

I've never wanted to be a piece of stainless steel before in my life... not up until now.

I shake the thought of being licked clean by Keely and keep on the conversation moving before the commercial breaks ends.

"You used to be a PT for a college football team? If I had had you as my PT in college, I think I might've tried to get injured on purpose just to see you," I say.

She tilts her head back and laughs. It's too early to be this addicted to her but it's too late.

I'm already hooked.

She points her spoon at me. "Nice try. You didn't go to college. You were drafted right out of high school."

"Oh, is that right?" I ask, an eyebrow raised at her knowledge of my career. "And how did you know that?"

She rolls her eyes playfully. "That wasn't a tough one. Most Hawkeyes fans know your draft history."

Okay... I'll give her a pass.

"I guess you're right. But if I knew you were the PT for a college hockey team, I might have skipped the NHL for another four years," I tease, dipping my own spoon into the chocolate ice cream and taking a big bite.

"Oh please, you would not have put off your career for four years just to see me in the PT room, that's ridiculous. And besides, it would put us in the same position we are in now. We can't date since I'm your physical therapist. The college had an obvious rule against student athletes and staff."

"Well I'm not a student, though I'd be happy to learn anything you want to teach me." And I mean anything. "And the Hawkeyes don't have anything against players and staff. It wouldn't be an issue if, for example, you and I dated."

Her eyes shift from the commercial about the importance of deworming your pets annually and stares at me.

"Reeve, I'm your PT."

"I know, I'm just saying that it's not exactly a professional ethics issue if your employer doesn't care, right?"

"I don't know, I guess I'd have to think about that. And I don't have a permanent job with the Hawkeyes yet. Plus, I still have a lot on my plate with this move to Seattle. I'm not in a good place to consider dating anyone."

Right now isn't a great time for me either. I didn't want any distractions this season and now, if Dr. Morgan is right and I can't rehab this knee, a distraction like Keely will be the least of my issues. I'll be looking for a new career.

"I'm not trying to pressure you. We both have a lot to do over the next six weeks," I say.

"Exactly. Let's focus on getting you back on the ice."

"You're right. Do you want the last bite or ice cream? I saved a marshmallow for you."

She smiles over at me. "Sure, thanks." She dips her spoon in and scoops the last bite. "You said you grew up in Alaska."

"Yeah, I did."

"Then how did you end up playing hockey for a high school in Houston, Texas?"

A wide grin pulls at my lips.

"What?" she asks.

"You've been stalking me on the internet."

It's not a question--she might as well have just admitted it.

"Damn it," I hear her mutter to herself.

I got her.

"I..." she stutters, scrambling for a cover. "It's part of my job to know your injury history, and since I don't have a medical file on you yet, I had to get what I could."

"What does my medical history have to do with where I grew up and where I went to high school?" I ask.

She diverts her attention back to the TV, and I can almost see the gears turning in her head, trying to devise a better excuse.

"There's actually a lot of studies working to answer that question. Some research suggests that water purity and air quality could possibly play a big enough role in bone density as a child. Stronger bones lead to less injury."

She's grasping for straws and we both know it.

"Hey, Doc..." I say, pulling her attention back. Her eyes meet mine--we both know I won this round. "If you had a Wikipedia page about you, I would have already read every word."

"Yeah, well, physical therapists don't typically have those," she shoots back.

"I know. I already looked."

Even with only the blue light of the TV casting a glow across Keely's face, I can see the blush warm on her cheeks.

"You looked me up?" she asks, genuine surprise in her voice.

"I tried. I couldn't find anything on Keely Woods," I say. "Unless it's under something else. You're not secretly married or something, are you?"

Her eyes widen, and for a moment, she looks like she's forgotten to breathe. But then I see the softness in her eyes when she realizes I'm joking.

She shakes her head. "No, I'm not secretly married. Just an ordinary PT with a passion for ice cream and a knack for proving you wrong."

"Well, the PT and ice cream are true at least," I say, unable to suppress a smile. "I guess you're just a mystery that I'll have to discover myself."

Keely lets out a yawn, her eyes fluttering, and she attempts to keep them open with limited success.

It's been a long day for both of us, and a little rest would be good.

I set the empty carton of ice cream on the coffee table nearby, and we polished it off.

Before I know it, Keely falls asleep, her head against my shoulder, and it's not long before my eyelids are too heavy to keep open.

Keely

I wake in a panic to the sound of Reeve groaning in pain.

"Reeve... Reeve," I say, rubbing my hand gently over his chest.

His eyes burst open to my voice. "Huh?" he says, almost like I woke him from a nightmare, and he doesn't know where he is.

"You're in your apartment with me. Are you in pain?" I ask.

He grimaces and then nods. He's still groggy from sleep and whatever I woke him from.

"Are you sure you don't want anything? Even Tylenol? Just a little something to help take the swelling down?" I ask.

I still have no idea what he has against pain meds but he's in so much pain right now that I just want to get him comfortable.

"No, I'll be okay. I just need another ice pack."

It's not what I was hoping to hear but this is his choice at the end of the day. However, it's easier to heal when you're not always tensing up in pain.

"Come on, let's get you in bed so you can stretch out. I'll bring your pillows in, prop you up and get you another ice pack."

It isn't long before I get Reeve into bed and settled. Once the new ice pack gets his knee numb again, he falls asleep.

I leave his bedroom door open so I can listen for him, and then I fall back to sleep on the couch.

I don't know what happened to make Reeve swear off even over-the-counter painkillers, but I have to find something else to help manage his pain if we're going to be able to jump into physical therapy.

Tomorrow, I'll start my research.

Chapter Nine

Keely

I fill Paula in on all the new developments with Reeve, mostly about the lack of pain meds while standing in the kitchen. With Reeve still asleep, I attempt to keep my voice down.

"Reeve may be feeling overwhelmed. Pain medication can make people feel vulnerable. It's not uncommon for athletes like him to want to push through the discomfort. And maybe he's telling the truth that pain meds dull his senses. That wouldn't be the first time I've heard an athlete say that. Though I've never experienced any of my post-surgery patients refusing drugs before–that's a first."

"Exactly! This can't be good for him to try to recover from this much pain. And how am I supposed to push him through strengthening techniques if he's in extreme pain while we do them?"

"Are you worried about his discomfort? Or yours?"

I wasn't expecting that question from her.

I'm a physical therapist and my job is to help people restore their mobility after an injury or surgery. My patients are usually always in some kind of discomfort during the process. But maybe she's right. Maybe seeing him in that much pain bothers me on a level that it never has before because of this inconvenient crush.

"It can be challenging in our line of work to push people through pain, especially when we feel something for them--"

"I don't feel anything for him. That would be inappropriate." I tell her.

I can practically hear her smile over the receiver.

"Okay... you don't have feelings for him. But remember that he is the only one who knows his own pain tolerance."

"Well, instead of allowing him to max out his pain tolerance, I've read about alternative ways to manage pain that aren't drug-related. Have you used anything like that with patients?"

"There are a few that can be effective, but it depends on the patient."

"Okay, so, like acupuncture and herbal remedies?"

"Yes, but there are a few others that he could try. Hypnosis, aromatherapy, meditation, sex..."

I just about swallow my own tongue with her last option.

"Did you just say sex?"

I've heard of the other ones in school, but sex is new.

"Yes, some patients find that having an orgasm serves as not only a distraction from the pain, but it has also been reported that patients benefit from the burst of endorphins which help to mask the pain. It doesn't work for everyone."

"Keely... are you here?" I hear Reeve's voice.

"Yeah, I'm here," I call back.

"He just woke up, I should check on him. Thanks for the advice Paula, I'll discuss a couple of the options with him and see if he wants to try any of them."

"Keep me posted, okay? I'm just a call away," Paula said before hanging up.

Taking a deep breath after that call, I head for Reeve's room.

I push through the open door and see Reeve standing with his crutches in the same clothes as yesterday.

"Hey, I didn't know if you had left already to pack for the new apartment."

"Nope. You have me until the superintendent comes by to change the locks. Then I'll run home and grab what I need. I don't have much anyway. I only packed a couple of suitcases just in case things didn't work out in Seattle."

Not like I have any intentions of going back.

I actually like working at my uncle's bar if finding a job in the field I want doesn't come quickly. Though I'm hoping that my agreement with the Hawkeyes all works out: Reeve will be back on the ice and I'll secure my dream job as the new PT on staff.

"I'd like to take a shower. I haven't taken one since after our win a couple of nights ago," he says, moving toward the ensuite in his bedroom.

I follow behind him until we're both standing in the bathroom.

"What's that?" he asks, pointing to the shower walker that I put in there yesterday.

"It's for stability while you shower. It was another one of the things I picked up based on the email I got from your doctor. Since you can't submerge your incision, you can't take a bath, and Dr. Morgan stressed very heavily that falling on your knee at this delicate time in your recovery could end your career."

The weight of my words feels heavy between us. Heavier than any conversation we've had so far, but he doesn't say anything back, he just stares at the walker for a second longer than I would expect him to. Maybe mentioning a career-ending fall was a step too far, but he needs to understand how serious this is, if he didn't already know.

"It's not forever, Reeve. Don't think on it for too long."

He nods and then I walk around him toward the shower, turning it on so that the water can start warming up.

"I appreciate everything you're doing. I hope you know that. You didn't have to stay last night... but I'm glad you did."

"You're welcome. And anyway... I owe you," I say, returning to him once the shower gets warmer.

"You don't owe me anything. It was an accident."

I just shrug to keep the emotion from welling up in my eyes.

It's hard to see him like this and not have guilt.

If he hadn't walked me out to my car, this wouldn't have happened to him. It would have been me instead and he'd be getting ready for today's home game.

"Do you want me to help you undress?"

A smirk creeps over Reeve's full lips. "Are you showering with me, Doc? Not that I mind if you want to watch. I've been traded to enough teams in my career that half the NHL has seen me naked at this point."

My belly flips with the idea of showering with Reeve... especially if he wasn't injured.

I clear my throat and shake away the mental picture of physical contact with a man like Reeve. It's been a while since the last time I was pushed up against a shower wall, and I'm definitely due.

"Oh darn, and here I thought I was special."

His eyes dart between mine. "You had it right the first time. You are special," he says.

I try not to squirm where I stand, showing evidence that his words affect me.

"Well even so, I'm not showering with you. I'm just going to be close by in case you start to slip. And I promise you, I'm a professional. But just to put your mind at ease, you're not the first patient I've seen naked."

His eyebrows raise in surprise. "Ouch Keely, that one dug deep. So, you mean to tell me I'm not the special one?" he says, gripping his shirt over his heart.

I roll my eyes. "Every one of my patients is my favorite."

I walk over, searching for a towel, and find a stack of folded towels under the sink and pull one out, dropping it onto the counter..

"Isn't that what all PT's say? Like when you ask your parents who their favorite child is?"

"Oh and I'm guessing you assume that you're the favorite in your family?" I ask.

He winces briefly at my question but recovers quickly like he didn't want me to see that and then covers it up with his charming smile. "Of course I'm my parent's favorite. They had me and then stopped when they knew they had made perfection. A second child would have been obsolete."

I snicker. "Lightning never strikes twice."

"Exactly, and I'm going to be your favorite, Keke. Just wait," He hobbles slowly toward the shower to get closer. "And by the way, I don't think any PT I've ever worked with has seen me naked, so I have to ask you... what's your number? And be careful what you say next. I might get jealous." he teases.

"My number? You mean the number of patients I've seen naked?" I ask.

He nods, reaching out to test the spray of the shower to test the temperature himself.

"I don't know how many. I never kept count, but I've seen patients naked plenty of times."

"Really, when?" he asks.

"In college they were cadavers."

He chuckles at my admission. "I knew it. I'm your first, huh?"

I step closer, gripping the hem of his t-shirt. My gaze flicks up to his for a moment, seeking consent. He nods, and I slowly lift the shirt.

"Yes, my first naked patient. But don't let it go to your head."

"If you're worried about me getting a big head, I wouldn't recommend looking down."

Despite my best intentions, my eyes drift down Reeve's sculpted torso, tracing the defined grooves leading to the deep V of his pelvis, where dark wisps of his happy trail tease just above the waistband of his gym shorts.

God, this man is stunning.

The thought of what lies beneath that fabric sends a thrill through me, and I remind myself firmly that I'm his physical therapist and nothing more.

And then my attention catches on something else.

Purple and yellow bruising on the side of his body peeks out of his shorts and past his hip bone. It's where he took the largest hit from the grill of the hit-and-run vehicle.

"Reeve..." I say, trying to mask the crack in my voice as emotion wants to break through.

He hooks a finger under my chin and gently lifts so that my focus turns up to meet his gaze.

"It's just a bruise. I get them every day at work. It'll fade," he pulls his finger back, gripping the crutch again. "I'd rather we keep doing what we were doing."

Heat floods my cheeks as I reach out, sliding his shorts down his legs while ensuring the waistband doesn't touch his injured knee. "Let's concentrate on keeping you from slipping in the shower instead of your... exhibitionist tendencies."

As soon as his shorts hit the ground, my eyes widen in shock. I was not prepared for Reeve's impressive size.

My jaw nearly drops as I take in the sight of him fully undressed in front of me.

It's been too long since the last time I was with a man. My reaction to Reeve makes it entirely evident.

"Fair enough," he says, pulling me from my gawking. "But just so we're clear, you didn't have to go as far as getting me in the shower if you wanted to see it—"

"Stop," I cut him off, laughter attempting to bubble out of my throat as I try to block it with the back of my hand.

Be professional for the love of God, Keely.

"This is serious, and if you fall while under my supervision—likely ending your career for good—Coach Bex will probably cut the brakes to my car," I warn.

I saw the look in Coach Bex's eyes when he gave me the deadline. He wants his player back and I could tell that he wasn't completely convinced that I'm the PT for the job. The look he gave me before we left the hospital was stern but hopeful.

Reeve's gaze roams over my body, taking in the way his oversized t-shirt hangs loose over my silhouette, the way his rolled-up boxers give me almost no curves, but even still, the way he's looking at me has my center clenching.

"Are you really wearing that into the shower?" he asks.

A blush creeps up my cheeks. "I don't have anything else to wear. Even if my luggage had made it, I definitely didn't pack a bathing suit for Seattle in the fall."

Reeve nods, his expression softening. "Okay," he says, turning away from me. His muscles tense as he pulls his crutches from under his arms and sets them against the glass shower door. He grips the shower walker tightly on both sides; determination etched on his face as he maneuvers himself into the shower without a hitch.

"Take your time," I say, stepping closer to the edge of the shower, my hands outstretched, wanting to be near in case he starts to slip.

He steps into the hot spray of the shower, a sigh passing through his lips, his shoulders relaxing as the warmth envelops him.

I can see the tension in his body begin to melt away.

I watch from the outside of the shower as the hot water cascades down his back and perfect glutes. I remember that first night we met at the bar—the spark between us igniting in playful banter and being wrapped up in his hoodie, feeling safer than I have in a long time. I didn't realize just how safe I actually was being with Reeve.

I know everything about being in the bathroom with him is dangerous to my plans to protect him from my father's sins, but I can't help myself from wanting to be closer.

I pull off my t-shirt and shorts and step onto the tile of the walk-in shower.

I'm still wearing my heather gray sports bra that zips up in the front, paired with matching boy shorts. While it's far from the most erotic outfit I could have chosen, comfort was my priority when I slipped these on yesterday morning for running errands. I hadn't anticipated the possibility of sharing a shower with the hot Hawkeyes goalie. To be honest, I haven't invested in many sexy bra sets since my last breakup three years ago with my ex, Owen, the golf pro who dumped me at his agent's suggestion. But it's just as well that I am not wearing see-through lace because the last thing I should be doing right now is seducing my patient.

The best thing I can do for Reeve is to remember why I'm here.

I'm here to prove that Dr. Morgan is wrong, and I have every intention of doing it. But as I step into the warm cascade, the steam envelops me, and the spicy scent of his body wash mingling with the hot water sends my mind reeling. Reeve steals a glance over his shoulder when he realizes I'm behind him, and the way his eyes narrow on me and then dip down my entire body ignites a burn within me that I wish I could stomp out.

"You know I was just kidding, right? You don't have to be in here with me. I can handle a shower on my own."

"I told you, if you fall, I'll have twenty-two large hockey players out looking for me. I'd have to join some kind of witness protection program."

"I get that you're kidding... but you should know I'll never let anyone hurt you."

I nod, biting down on my lip, and then a moment of silence passes between us. The sound of the shower spray hitting the metal walker and Reeve's body are the only noises breaking the stillness. Water cascades down, producing a soothing rhythm as droplets splatter against the porcelain tiles.

He turns back to the shower, reaching for the body wash sitting on a small, tiled shelf in front of him, squeezing enough into his hand, and then starts to rub his arms and chest with the spicy fragrant soap.

"Are you really planning to just stand there?" he teases, breaking the tension in the air. "Because I could use a hand. Or two."

"This is a shower, Reeve, not a swim lesson, and I plan to keep my hands to myself unless it comes down to preventing a career-ending slip."

"I guess that means a simple reach-around is out of the question? Duly noted." A soft chuckle escapes him and cuts through the seriousness of our current situation, reminding me why I feel so drawn to him in the first place. "Well, then, I could use some educational assistance on careful shower techniques." His playful challenge hangs in the air, tantalizing enough to encourage me to step closer.

He glances back over his shoulder at me when he senses that I'm drawing closer.

"Keely, I'm not serious. I'm just lightening the mood. You don't have to do anything."

"I know, but the least I can do is get your back. Can you hand me the soap?" I ask.

Is it wrong for me to take this opportunity to touch him?

Maybe nothing more can happen between us, but I can at least help him after he's done so much for me.

"Are you sure?" he asks.

"I'm sure."

Taking a deep breath, I maneuver my arm around him, staying focused as best as I can on his safety as I take the bottle of soap that he's handing me.

I take the bottle, squeezing more product into my hand than I meant to. The bottle becomes so slippery that I can't hold onto it any longer and it slides right out, dropping onto the tiled shower and making a loud noise and spilling some of the soap on the ground.

I yelp and jump at the sound but when I come down, I slip on the soap.

Before I have a chance to hit the ground, a strong arm reaches around my waist and yanks me up against hard, fresh muscles.

"Reeve! No!" I say, knowing he could lose his balance and slip along with me.

He pulls me over to the tile wall—a groan of pain slips through his lips and my stomach twists at the thought that I just re-injured him.

Oh God... and I'll have to take him back to Dr. Morgan and somehow explain that we were showering together, and I caused his re-injury. I took an oath to do no harm, and here we are.

I don't even want to think of what Coach Bex and Sam will say about this.

"You should have let me fall," I say, my hands against his shoulders as I'm caught between a shower wall, Reeve's thick chest and his hard cock pressed between us against my belly.

A shiver of need rolls up my spine as the heat from his erection radiates against me.

He drops his forehead to mine--his eyes closed as his breathing labors in pain-- his left forearm leans against the wall behind me to balance him while his other arm is still protectively holding me to him.

I thought that I couldn't feel worse than when I saw Reeve in the hospital after the car hit him, but now I've caused him more pain that could have been avoided if I had just let him shower alone.

I'm his physical therapist for God Sake.

My hands trace up his neck until my arms wrap around his neck. "I'm so sorry, Reeve. I didn't mean to hurt you. The soap--and then the water--and I slipped--"

"Shhh," he says gently, and when his eyes open, the golden amber of his iris locks on mine. There's still pain in his eyes but it's softening. "I'm okay. I've played through worse. Besides, I'd take any injury for this. I'd never pass up a chance to hold you."

There's no teasing smirk across his lips.

No playful banter.

He means every word.

The boldness of his confession jars me, making my heart skip a beat. I'm torn, caught between the professional responsibility to help him heal and a stronger urge to lean into this connection pulling me in.

"I want you to hold me too," I admit, hesitating to allow myself to give in, but he's making it impossible to hold back.

Suddenly, Reeve's lips crash against mine in a desperate kiss, unleashing a rush of heat and need between us. I melt into his embrace, surrendering to the need I've tried to suppress.

My fingers tangle in his damp hair as his tongue slides across my lips, asking for consent. I open for him, allowing him access to deepen our kiss.

His hand that was once curled around my back trails up the side of my body, caressing my curves the way I've imagined he would since the night we met. I gasp as his fingers skim the edge of my sports bra, our kiss growing more urgent and demanding. Desire pulses through me, urging me to give in to temptation despite the voice in the back of my mind telling me that I should stop this, but I can't.

I'm drunk on his kiss and no longer thinking about the consequences.

"Keely..." he growls against my parted lips, his voice tinged with urgency. "I want to touch you. I've wanted it since the moment I first saw you."

My heart pounds against my rib cage and I know he can feel it too.

I should tell him "no". I should protect us both from the possibility of mixed signals and hook-ups that won't go anywhere because I can't bring myself to taint his budding career. But I can't deny him.

Maybe I could have if he wasn't working his way down my throat, kissing and sucking and nibbling his way to my collarbone.

Maybe I could say no if the thick tip of his cock wasn't pressing against my stomach, making me think of how good he'd fill me.

I nod encouragingly, granting him silent permission.

His hand comes between us, flattening against my soft belly and sliding gently down until his fingers find the waistband of my boy shorts, slipping into my slick folds as I grip tighter around his neck.

I choke out a sound of pleasure as he strokes my sensitive flesh, coating his fingers in my arousal and using it to gently spread me open. He continues his testing and teasing until I can't help but rock into his hand the closer he takes me to the edge.

Each time his fingers stroke my clit, a million nerve endings explode like fireworks.

"Yes..." I hiss, my head falling back against the tiles. "Please, don't stop."

"I won't stop until I feel you squeeze my fingers. I want to feel you come."

He dips one finger inside of me and I take a deep inhale as I almost come right then.

"Does that feel good?" he asks, plunging another finger into my core.

I moan out his name, my arms tighten around his neck again, bringing him even closer than before. At this point we couldn't be any closer unless we were one person.

"So responsive," Reeve says, his praise unleashing renewed tingles at every nerve ending. "I can feel you tightening. You're close."

I nod against his shoulder--my ability to speak is completely gone. Arousal and need are the only things that live here anymore.

His fingers begin pumping deeper, steady thrusts until I'm clawing at his back. His thumb focuses pressure on my throbbing clit, setting off more sparks that heat low in my belly.

"I'm going to make you come so hard that you keep coming back for more. So that it's harder for you to make an excuse for why we can't date. I want you addicted to my fingers, Keke."

And then I come--crying out his name as the orgasm pulsates through every cell of my body.

He peppers kisses down my neck and shoulder as he holds me in place while he waits patiently for me to come down from the high.

I take a cleansing breath once my brain finally catches up with what just happened.

I peer down between us.

I can feel the tip of Reeve's cock pulsate against my skin. He has to be uncomfortably hard.

"What about you?" I ask, and then look down at the erection between us.

"Are you asking him or me?"

I glance up to find that teasing smirk across his lips again.

"I don't know, do you two have different answers?"

"Definitely," he says, brushing back a few wet strands of my hair and tucks them behind my ear. "But his opinion doesn't matter to me and it shouldn't matter to you."

"Really?" I ask, feeling a little guilty.

"Really. That was just a sample taste. If you want more... you have to give me more in return."

My eyebrows lift in question. "More like what?"

"For starters, you can drop the "we can't be together because I'm your PT" excuse."

"Reeve... I--"

A loud knock on the front door of the apartment echoes through the bathroom.

"My apartment key..." I say.

He lets out a frustrated sigh.

He knows I just got saved by the bell from having to further this conversation.

"Fine but I'm getting the key. He doesn't get to see you like this," he says, his eyes sweeping over my face.

"Like what?"

"Freshly finger fucked and looking drop-dead gorgeous."

Quickly, he and I work to get the shower turned off, a towel around his waist and his crutches in place.

As soon as he passes through his bedroom and out to the front door, I pull off my bra and underwear while he's getting the key and thanking the superintendent. I yank on my scrubs without anything underneath.

It's not the first time I've gone commando, and since I'm just running back to the apartment above my uncle's garage and then back here to the fully furnished apartment that the Hawkeyes rented for me, it's not a big deal.

Before I walk out the door, I glance at his unmade bed and think about how tonight I'll be staying in my own apartment and not right out in the living room where I can easily change his ice pack. An uneasy feeling settles in my stomach at the thought of Reeve being in his apartment alone.

I walk out of the bedroom and head for the kitchen, wanting to make sure to get him set up with pillows and an ice pack before I leave, though I'm hoping to avoid Reeve starting up the conversation about us dating.

If he cares about his career then he and I can't date. I'm not ready to tell him the truth about my dad, and the real reason for why he and I will never be anything more than PT and patient.

If I have a choice, Reeve will never find out about my dad. I couldn't stand Reeve seeing me differently than he does now.

The front door closes, and Reeve turns around with his crutches and sees me heading for the kitchen.

"Got it," he smiles, holding it up.

"Perfect, thanks," I say and then pull open the freezer, grabbing an ice pack out. "It might take a few hours and I need to run an errand or two but I'll bring back dinner before I head to Oakley's tonight to help out after the home game–" And then I realized what I just said.

Reeve's expression just barely drops and I know he's hiding his disappointment on my account, which I hate."Shoot, I'm sorry,"

"It sucks but it is what it is. I wish I could be at the game at least but Phil and Sam want me to stay home for a few more days to heal first. Sam told me that security has been advised not to let me in if I show up."

"Sounds like they know you very well and they're serious about you resting and healing. Do you want me to call someone to be here with you today or tonight?" I ask, walking the ice packs over to the living room and setting up the pillows that I left out here for him.

He heads in my direction, staring down at the pillows and the ice pack that I have set up for him.

"No, I'll be fine. Dinner would be great but you don't have to do that either if you're settling in next door."

"Is pizza okay? It's fast and there's a good place by my uncle's house."

"Sounds good to me."

We exchange phone numbers in case he needs me to pick anything up and then I'm out the door and headed for my uncle's place.

Chapter Ten

Reeve

After Keely leaves, I sit down on the couch and start icing my knee.

Missing tonight's game is the stark reality check that if I don't do everything I can to recover and rehab, then two nights ago might have been my last night as a professional hockey player.

Keely's right to say that my recovery should be our primary focus. If I want to play again, I need to put everything I have into getting back to playing at my highest level.

My phone rings and I glance down at the caller.

Dad calling...

"Hey pops," I say.

"Reeve. Hi, son. How are you feeling since I talked to you yesterday? You're home from the hospital, right?"

The last time we talked, I was still waiting in my hospital room to be discharged, and then last night, when he texted to check in, my phone was on silent while Keely and I spent the evening together.

"Yeah, and the Hawkeyes already hired me a physical therapist who they moved into the building to make sure I have the best shot at rehabbing my knee, so you don't need to pay for one, but I appreciate the offer."

Not that he would have needed to with the money I make, even if the Hawkeyes weren't covering it. But my dad did well for himself and he's always offering to pay for anything I need. Maybe it's his way of making up for not being in my life as much as we both wanted him to be.

He started out as a roughneck in Alaska at eighteen for an oil rigging company, and then by the time I was six, he had worked his way up the company far enough that they offered him a position to run his own oil field in Texas, and that's where he still lives with my stepmom, living in an upscale gated community, driving golf carts instead of vehicles around the premises.

"I know you don't like the idea, but what about an in-house caretaker? I could pay to have someone around to run errands and make food for you. Maybe do laundry... that sort of thing."

"I'm fine pops, I promise."

"You'll let me know if you change your mind?"

I can hear the worry in his voice.

"I will," I assure him.

"You're sure I shouldn't come out there? I could spend a couple of weeks or a month with you and--"

"I'm good, I swear. My teammates all live in the same building, and the PT now lives across the hall. I have more help than I can handle," I tell him to put his mind at ease.

Ever since I moved from Alaska to Texas when I was fourteen, he seems to think I won't communicate if I need help or if there's trouble. I guess our history might bring him to that conclusion.

"If your mom were still alive, she'd be there with you. She'd know what to do."

It's a nice memory to have of my mom, but in the end, she couldn't take care of herself, let alone me. He keeps her memory in the good lighting, and I appreciate it because that's where I like to keep her, too. But some of his reasoning is from the guilt he feels, though in all fairness, she left him.

"You're doing just fine, pops."

The phone goes static for a second.

"How are you doing with the pain meds?" he asks.

I knew he'd eventually ask—after all, it goes along with the history.

"I told them I didn't want any."

"Reeve..." he says with a sigh of disappointment. "Your mom's therapist shouldn't have said what she said to you. You were too young to be told those things. Whether an addictive tendency is written in your DNA or not, it doesn't mean you'll become an addict. Your mother had a series of unfortunate events that left her in pain all the time and she didn't seek out help as soon as she should have. That doesn't mean that you're predestined to become an addict. And if your mother knew that you denied pain meds because of her, she'd—"

"She'd ask the doctor to prescribe them anyway behind my back and tell them I changed my mind? Or steal the ones I did get from my medicine cabinet?"

I hate talking about her like this, which is why I don't talk about her much at all.

I like to remember all the ways that she nurtured my dreams as a hockey player and used every dollar my dad paid her in child support to pay for extra coaching, new equipment, and summer hockey camps. She drove me to every practice and sat in the stands for the entire duration. She didn't bring a tablet or a book with her. She'd just sit there watching every minute. She was my biggest fan.

I don't want to remember her as an addict because that's not who she was... but it doesn't mean her addiction hasn't shaped me into who I am now, because it has.

"I'm sorry I didn't see it, son. I'm sorry I wasn't there for you when you needed me to be--when both of you needed me."

My dad's constant guilt isn't fair, either.

He thought he was giving us a better life in Texas, but she didn't want the big house or the spending account.

She just wanted the same twenty-one-year-old roughneck man she married and a simple life in Alaska--the only home she had ever known.

"Actually, I changed my mind. We haven't seen each other in a while. I do want you to come. But how about Christmas in Seattle? Has Caroline ever had a snowy Christmas?"

Caroline is my stepmom and the honest-to-God nicest person I've ever met.

If you looked up Texas debutante in the dictionary, her picture would be right beside it. You'd also find her picture next to Southern Hospitality.

I know that a lot of people don't get along with their step-parents, but Caroline is impossible to hate. It would be like trying to hold a grudge against a Teletubby or a gummy bear.

If it's all an act, then she deserves a fucking Oscar because I haven't seen her slip up once over the eighteen-plus years I've known her.

"She'd love it! I'll have her start looking for a house rental for the weekend."

"Sounds good pops."

"I love you, Reeve."

"I love you too, dad."

I fill the rest of my day with research on past athletes who have had knee surgeries and came back to play professionally again. I know this is Keely's area of expertise, but I need something to fill my time and distract me from the fact that I should be heading into the stadium to warm up right about now, and instead, I can't even go down to at least be in the locker room with the guys tonight because Coach Bex and Sam don't trust that I won't reinjure myself.

When Keely shows back up to the apartment, my heart sinks at the t-shirt she's wearing. It has Oakley's logo on it, and it's just another reminder that even Keely gets to celebrate with my team, and I don't.

We eat the pizza she brought and I walk over to her new apartment with her to see the place. Or at least that's what I tell her, but in truth, I want to make sure she's safe and that there isn't anything wrong with the apartment.

It's a studio, so it's smaller than mine by an entire bedroom, but it's also temporary, and she says it's bigger than the place she has at Oakley's, so it's more than adequate for her needs. I'm just glad that it worked out and she is close by.

We head back to my apartment so she can get her purse and phone that she left and then she pulls out a baby monitor from the department store she went to today.

"Do we need to have the birds and bees talk? Because I only used my fingers this morning. And if you gauged my girth at only two fingers wide, then I'm mildly insulted."

"I'll never tell," she singsongs and then takes the baby monitor to my room.

The anticipation at what she plans on doing with that has my body thrumming with excitement and my brain firing off a million dirty images of Keely, me, and a camera.

Or shit... Keely and a camera would be fine too.

I make my way toward my bedroom to find Keely plugging the camera in and turning a switch on the top.

"I turned off the camera so that I can't see you on the other end, I can only hear you. And it's on mute so I can only hear you when you turn it on. I got it so that I can hear you tonight. If you need me, I can easily zip over and help," She looks down at her phone, her eyes flashing. "I have to go. I told my uncle I would be there a little early to help with inventory before the crowd hits at happy hour. Are you going to be okay while I'm gone?"

"I'll be fine, don't worry about me. I'll just be here icing my knee and learning about the mating ritual of the humpback whale."

"Spoiler alert, but did you know that the males engage in a weird ritual where they fight and try to push each other out of line behind the female? It's also rumored that ultimately females pick their mates and researchers believe that it's usually the larger, stronger, older males."

I stare back at her as she sets the camera next to my bed and checks the monitor to make sure it's working on her end.

"You just gave me a huge brain boner."

"Excuse me?" she chuckles.

"You're really smart, and it's freaking hot."

"Thank you," she smiles, a flicker of something in her eye. "And I think it's cute that out of everything you could watch on TV, that you watch the Discovery Channel."

"Cute?" I say with a scoff. "You have to do better than that."

"Okay, fine, I find it outrageously sexy that you choose to watch humpback whales doing it in your spare time."

"That's better."

She shakes her head and then heads toward me standing in my bedroom doorway.

"Now I really have to go. I'm going to drop the monitor off at my apartment and then I'm going to head to the bar. You might be asleep by the time I get home so make sure you turn on the monitor before you go to bed," she says.

"Okay," I say but my stomach knots up at the idea of her going to the bar without me there to walk her to her car.

"Hey, Keely?"

"Yeah?"

"Don't walk to your car alone. And make sure to look both ways."

Chapter Eleven

Keely

I drag myself through the door of my new apartment, exhausted but happy to have gotten to help my uncle after another busy night at Oakley's, with the Hawkeyes winning another game. The familiar scent of beer and greasy bar food clings to my clothes, a reminder of the energetic atmosphere I just left behind.

Kicking off my shoes, I pad across the room, my feet sinking into the plush carpet. The studio apartment may be small, but it already feels cozy and welcoming. I'm grateful for this space, a temporary home that brings me closer to my dreams—and to Reeve.

I shake my head, trying to dislodge thoughts of him. It's becoming harder to maintain professional boundaries when he's constantly on my mind.

Grabbing my sleepwear from the dresser, I head to the bathroom for a quick shower. The hot water washes away the grime and tension of the day but does little to calm my racing thoughts.

As I towel off and change, my eyes fall on the baby monitor sitting on my nightstand. A smile tugs at my lips, imagining Reeve on the other end, probably engrossed in another nature documentary. Or maybe he already fell asleep.

I crawl into bed, pulling the covers up to my chin. Just as I'm about to turn off the lamp, I hear his voice.

"Testing—testing—you there Keeks?" Reeve's voice sounds surprisingly crisp through the monitor with a new nickname to add to the pile.

I hit the button to let my voice through. "I'm here. I just got home a little bit ago and took a shower."

He lets out a sigh of relief. "I thought I heard an apartment door close down the hall. Glad to hear you are safe on the other end. Is it stupid that I was up all night worried about you?"

My heart squeezes at his admission. "It's not stupid, just unnecessary. I don't know if you put out an ABP, but the team wouldn't let me so much as scratch my own nose with less than three of them watching my every move."

"Sorry. I guess they took it seriously when I told them that if a single strand of hair on your head gets injured tonight, I'll take a bat to my bum knee."

I giggle, knowing full well that he wouldn't actually go through with that, it's a little dramatic but I doubt he actually told the guys that. My guess is that he saves the theatrics just for me. But the thought was sweet, hinting that my safety is more important than his career. And I guess he's already proven that based on the fact that he's lying in his bed across the hall with an ice pack on his knee and half of the right side of his body is bruised.

"Well, I appreciate the concern, but I promise I can take care of myself, though my uncle walked me out to my car himself this time. He says he drives around during the day when the bar is closed and looks for sedans with a smashed-in front end that looks like they hit a six foot three, two hundred and forty-pound hockey player. How are you feeling? Did you ice your knee like we discussed?"

"Yes, Ma'am," Reeve replies, a hint of amusement in his voice. "I've been a good patient, following doctor's orders to the letter."

"I'm impressed," I tease. "And here I thought I'd have to wrestle you into compliance."

There's a pause, and when Reeve speaks again, his voice is lower, more intimate. "You know, if you wanted to wrestle me, Doc, all you had to do was ask. Just be forewarned, I took first place in my weight class at my high school's state wrestling championship in my senior year."

"In your dreams, Aisa," I retort, trying to keep my voice light.

"Oh, you have no idea," he chuckles, the sound rich and warm through the monitor.

I curl onto my side, clutching a pillow to my chest. "So, what thrilling documentary did you watch tonight? More whale mating rituals?"

"Actually, I switched it up. Learned all about the courtship of emperor penguins. Did you know they're monogamous and mate for life?"

I smile at his enthusiasm for animal facts. It's endearing how much a brawny hockey player enjoys learning about nature.

"I did know that, actually. They're quite romantic for birds, aren't they? The male even incubates the egg while the female goes off to feed."

"Look at you whipping out animal facts all willy-nilly like some kind of hot zoologist," Reeve says, his voice warm with admiration. "I can already imagine you in a pair of sexy khaki shorts and hiking boots. Please tell me you have a pair."

"Of course I do," I say, deciding to play along.

"Please tell me you're wearing them now," he says in a sexy bedtime voice that's doing more for me than it should, considering he's only teasing.

"I'm rolling on my calf-height wool socks now," I tell him.

"Oh God, I'm going to come," he chokes out.

"I'm glad you're so easy."

I hear the deep rumble of his laugh. It's smooth but raspy at the same time. The kind of sound that makes me clench my thighs together.

"You could be the elephant poop scooper, and I'd still line up to take you home at the end of the workday--after I hose you down first. I mean, don't get it twisted Keke, I'm not just after your brains. I like your body too," he teases.

"So eloquent and genteel--and wildly generous with your compliments. It's a wonder that some lucky lady hasn't snatched you up already." I can already imagine the wide grin across his lips. "And although I appreciate all the new career prospects you've given me to consider, I think I'll stick to physical therapy."

"Disappointing, but a good choice."

"Speaking of which, how's the pain tonight? There are alternative methods for pain management that we haven't discussed yet."

There's a pause, and I can almost picture him considering it. "I'm managing with the ice at this point. No need to mess with what works."

I bite my lip, torn between respecting his wishes and wanting to do more to help. "Okay, but promise me you'll tell me if it gets too bad? We can always explore other options."

"I promise," he says. "You know, having you just across the hall... it helps more than you know."

My breath catches at his words, warmth spreading through my chest. "I'm glad I can help, even if it's just by being nearby."

We fall into a comfortable silence for a moment, and I find myself wishing I could see his face--read his expression.

"Keely?" Reeve's voice breaks the quiet, sounding hesitant.

"Yeah?"

"Thank you. For everything. I don't know what I'd do without you here."

I swallow hard, fighting the urge to rush across the hall and wrap my arms around him and let him engulf me in kisses. But instead, I close my eyes, willing my heart to slow its frantic beating. "Get some rest, okay? We've got a lot of work to do over the next six weeks and sleep is good for healing."

"Yes, ma'am," he says, and I can hear the smile in his voice. "Sweet dreams, Doc."

"Sweet dreams, Reeve," I whisper back, my finger lingering on the button before I release it.

I lay there for a long time until I finally fall asleep.

Chapter Twelve

Keely

I stir awake to the sound of Reeve groaning softly in his room coming through the baby monitor.

Intently I listen to the monitor as the pained sounds continue.

"Reeve..." I say softly, but I don't receive a reply.

My heart aches hearing him suffer as the groaning continues.

"Reeve, are you awake?" I ask a little louder this time.

After a few moments of internal debate, I decide I can't just listen to this anymore. I need to check on him.

I get up out of bed, head for the island where I dropped both of the keys for his apartment and mine and then I unlock my apartment door and head straight for his. I already know he's asleep and since I don't want to wake the neighbors with my loud knocking, I use my key to enter his apartment.

I knew I should have slept on the couch tonight, but after what happened yesterday morning in the shower, I knew it would be easy to have an encore if I had.

I walk up to Reeve's closed bedroom door. Knocking softly, I call out, "Reeve? Are you okay?"

There's a pause, then his groggy voice responds, "Keely?"

"Yeah, it's me. I heard you on the monitor."

"You can come in," he says.

I push the door open gently. In the dim light, I can see Reeve lying in bed, his face tight with discomfort.

"I'm fine. I forgot to get a new ice pack before I fell asleep after talking to you and the pain woke me up."

"You don't seem fine," I say gently. "But let me get you a fresh ice pack before I assess you."

I head to the kitchen and grab a new ice pack from the freezer. When I return, Reeve has managed to sit up slightly in bed.

"Here," I say, carefully placing the ice pack on his knee. "This should help numb things a bit."

Reeve winces slightly but then relaxes as the cold takes effect. "Thanks," he murmurs, the tension in his shoulders easing.

I hover over him for a moment. "Do you need anything else? Water? More pillows?"

He shakes his head. "No, I'm okay. You can go back to sleep. I'm sorry I woke you up."

"It's fine. I want you to wake me when you're in pain so that I can help," I say. "I'm going to sleep on the couch tonight so that I'm close. Just call out if you need me for anything."

But as I turn to leave, his hand reaches out and gently grasps my wrist. "Actually...would you mind staying? Just until I fall asleep again?"

The vulnerability in his voice tugs at my heart. Against my better judgment, I nod. "Of course."

I sit on the edge of the bed and then lay down beside him. We lay there in comfortable silence for a while, the only sound his gradually steadying breathing.

Just as I think he's drifted off, Reeve speaks softly. "My mom died when I was fourteen."

His admission takes me by surprise. "You were so young," I say.

I look over to find Reeve staring up at the ceiling--his eyes deary and sad--his lips pressed into a thin line.

"She and I were in a car accident when I was five," he continues quietly. "I only broke my arm but she sustained more injuries and needed multiple surgeries after that. Some of the surgeries were successful, but others weren't and only caused her more pain."

I listen intently, sensing this is something he doesn't share often. My heart aches for the young boy who went through such trauma.

"The doctors kept prescribing her pain medication. No one knew how bad it was getting, not even me," Reeve says. "At first it helped, but then it became something else entirely. She tried rehab a couple of times but it never stuck. Then years after the accident, I got my first bad hockey injury and my doctor prescribed me pain meds. I thought I was being forgetful about taking them when I noticed that the bottle seemed to dwindle faster than it should have, but I was just a kid. The next summer, I broke my collarbone on a rope swing, and the same thing happened. I still didn't put it all together."

"How could you have? You were just a kid."

He shakes his head as if he's still trying to think of what he missed with her like the signs were there.

"After that, she started seeing a therapist and within a few weeks she had checked into rehab. That was the first time. After she got out, I denied pain meds whenever a doctor prescribed them."

I hold my breath, already sensing what's coming next. I already want to wrap my arms around the eight-year-old Reeve, who had to handle such a difficult situation.

He takes a shaky breath. "She died of liver failure when I was fourteen. That's why I stopped taking pain meds."

"What about your dad? Was he in the picture?"

He nods. "My parents divorced when I was four after my dad got a promotion that required a move to Texas, but my mom never warmed up to the place-- she missed the mountains and her family. Six months later, she packed me up and took me back. I spent the school year with her and a month in the Texas summer with my dad."

"That must have been an adjustment?"

"I spent every minute I could at the local ice rink practicing with the Zamboni driver until his wife made him come home for dinner."

I laugh--that sounds like Reeve.

"So the obsession with hockey isn't new?"

"It's more like an addiction; I've just learned how to channel it."

"Reeve..." I start.

He turns his head against the pillow, and those warm eyes that I'm finding harder and harder to say no to settle on me.

"I'm sorry I dumped all of that on you. This surgery has brought up stuff that I haven't thought about in a really long time. It's not something I usually fixate on."

I nod, understanding that having to manage the pain has brought some other hurt to the surface.

"You can tell me anything you want."

"I know. You can tell me anything you want, too."

I lick my lips and then give a polite smile, which he accepts and then turns his eyes back up to the ceiling.

But the truth is, I can't tell him anything I want. Not if I want to avoid him seeing me as a virus to his long-desired career.

Hockey is what kept him sane all those years. The moment the sponsors start backing out and teams don't want to take a chance with him on the roster because of his girlfriend's father, he'll resent me, and I'll resent myself.

"Thank you for sharing that with me," I say softly. "I understand now. We'll find other ways to manage your pain, I promise."

Reeve turns his head to look at me, a small smile on his lips despite the sadness in his eyes. "You said earlier that there are other options?"

Remembering my earlier conversation with Paula, I debate how many of the options I should give him. "Yes, there are some alternative methods we could try. Things like acupuncture, meditation, aromatherapy..."

I trail off, debating whether to mention the last option Paula suggested. Reeve raises an eyebrow, noticing my hesitation.

"There's more?" he says.

I feel my cheeks warm slightly. "Well, um, there's also...sex."

His eyes widen in surprise. "Sex?"

"Yeah," I say, trying to keep my voice casual. "Some studies have shown that orgasms can help with pain management. The endorphin release acts as a natural painkiller."

Reeve is quiet for a moment, and I worry I've made things awkward. But then a small smirk tugs at his lips.

"So you're saying doctor's orders are for me to have more orgasms?" he teases. "I like that option... how do we explore it?" His eyes twinkle with amusement.

"Do you actually think that sex would work?" he asks.

"I'm not sure, but I have to admit that I'm curious."

"Just come out with it, Doc. Are you asking me to be your sexy little science experiment?"

I turn my body toward him, laying on my side to face him, my hands curling up under the pillow below my head.

"There's nothing little about you, Reeve."

"Good point. So true." He grins back at me.

His hand slips between my waist and the mattress as he hooks his arm around my back, pulling me flush against his side. My hand settles on his chest, and my leg instinctively curls over the top of his uninjured knee, maybe because being close to him comes more naturally than I'm willing to admit.

"So, we'll call it a science experiment. A one-time thing to test out the theory."

"Is that code for "no-strings-attached"? Because we both know that an experiment takes more than one time to test thoroughly, and I hypothesize that one time won't be enough." Reeve's hand slips further down my lower back until his fingertips skim teasingly at the skin above my pajama bottoms. "I'm very thorough when it comes to my research."

He pulls me closer--A shiver rolls through me as his eyes dip down to my lips.

"It shouldn't be too hard to prove. All you have to do is tell me if you're still in pain after you come inside me."

Reeve's eyes go hooded with desire instantly.

"Jesus, Keely," he says, his eyes dilating just before his lips crash against mine--the taste of need so sweet on his tongue as he gains access to my mouth--his hand dips beneath my waistband, squeezing my ass cheek and pulling me tighter against his thigh.

I moan at the feeling of pressure against my needy clit.

My body begins to grind against his leg like the desperate, sex-deprived woman that I am. A deep growl rumbles through his chest--his hand encouraging me to grind faster, harder. "That's it. Just like that."

He pulls his hand from my ass cheek--both hands gripping around my waist, pulling me up until I'm straddling his leg. My hands flatten against his chest as if to anchor me in place as I pick up my pace. I feel the wetness between my thighs soak my panties, and I wonder if he can feel the moisture through my pajama bottoms.

"This isn't what we agreed to--me coming like this," I say because there's no hiding the fact from either of us. He has me on the edge and I won't last much longer before I come with both of us still fully clothed.

"I need you dripping wet first before you take me. I don't want to hurt you."

More liquid arousal spills into my panties at the thought of how far Reeve's cock will stretch me open.

His hand dips under the front of my shorts--his thumb rolling and presses against my already throbbing clit, pulling a whimper from my lips.

"Reeve... I'm--" I choke out in a warning, my fingernails digging into his chest as my center begins to squeeze while he plays with my tender nub.

And then I scream out my orgasm, bracing myself against his chest to keep myself from crashing against his chest.

My eyes find his--he's been watching me.

We're not done.

Not even close.

"You're gorgeous when you come, did you know that?" he asks, his honest eyes searching mine.

I shake my head.

I've never been told that after sex, but it's no surprise that with Reeve, everything is different.

And now more than anything, I want to know what he feels like inside of me.

"I want you, Reeve," I tell him.

It's the first time I've ever said those words out loud to him.

"Finally," he says and reaches up for me.

Before I know it, we're in a mad rush, stripping each other bare of every inch of clothing.

Gym shorts, pajama bottoms, panties, and then my shirt--all tossed onto the wood floors of his bedroom until there's nothing between us but skin

His eyes roam over my bare breasts and down my torso and then to my bare pussy, his gaze appreciative.

His hands come up, gliding over my hard nipples before he cups my breasts--I hum in approval that I like the way his hands feel.

I watch as he reaches for a condom on the nightstand by his head. Pulling one out, he rips the foil and rolls it on.

I lift my leg to straddle him, and he guides me slowly until he lines me up with his tip.

"You'll tell me if I'm going too fast or if I'm hurting your knee, right?"

He chuckles as if the idea is preposterous. "Hurt me Keely. Do your best."

I line myself up with him, rubbing the head of his cock through my slick folds. Then, with one swift movement, I sink down onto him, taking him slowly at first, letting my body adapt to his girth--my body stroking his length as groans of pleasure pass through his lips, until I take one last thrust, taking all of him until he bottoms out inside of me.

"Oh fuck," Reeve groans, his head falling back against the pillow. "You feel incredible."

I start to move again, but Reeve takes control, gripping my hips and guiding my movement until I'm riding him hard and fast. The pleasure is so intense, it's bordering on too much, but I refuse to hold back.

"You ride my cock so well," he mutters.

His hand reaches up behind my neck and pulls me down against his lips, my breasts pressing against his chest as he sets our pace--his cock stroking over and over against the hot button inside of me that he knows just how to press. Reeve releases my lips and pulls me higher until his lips find my puckered nipple.

His lips suction around me while his tongue playfully flicks and licks my needy nub until I'm melting into him.

"I'm so close," I pant, begging him with my hips to increase the tempo. "Faster, Reeve, please don't stop."

Reeve doubles his efforts, thrusting his hips up to meet my strokes. But then I hear his grunts of pain. "Reeve, stop! Your knee," I beg, but he doesn't stop; he only increases his rhythm. The coil of pleasure in my belly snaps and I come careening back to earth, my walls fluttering and pulsating around Reeve's cock.

"That's it, Keely," Reeve praises, continuing to stroke me through my orgasm. "You're so perfect."

A few more hard thrusts and Reeve is coming too, spilling himself deep inside me with a guttural moan. I collapse against his chest, both of us gasping for breath.

"That was..." Reeve starts but can't find the words.

"Pain relieving?" I tease.

"The results were inconclusive. Looks like we'll have to try again."

"Too bad we already agreed to one time," I say, though I wish there was a chance for more.

I push up off his chest and move to the edge of the bed, reaching down to grab my shirt and pull it on.

"Hey, where are you going?"

"To set up the couch for tonight."

"You said that you would stay with me until I fell asleep."

"That's true, I did.

He holds open his arms and I lay back down

Hours after we both fall asleep, I wake and realize that I'm getting too comfortable with Reeve. It's time for a little distance, even if it's the last thing I want.

Chapter Thirteen

Reeve

A text chimes on my phone and though I always want it to be Keely, I know it won't be since she's at the bar doing inventory with Oakley.

> Seven: Gym?

A man of few words.

> Reeve: Sure sounds good. When?

> Seven: 15

I'm guessing he means in 15 minutes, but if he means 15 hours... I'll still be doing nothing and available to go.

> Reeve: I'll be ready.

Getting out of this apartment and into the stadium is just what I need today. Sam and Coach Bex imposed a one-week hiatus for me to ensure that I would take it easy and heal up, but now I just want to get back to work.

It's been almost a week since Keely fell asleep in my arms after the night we had sex, but by the time I woke in the morning, she was up making breakfast, and I found a blanket and a pillow on the couch. While I was out cold, she moved like she said that she would. We didn't discuss it and I pretended not to notice.

Now, I'm sitting on the couch, my leg propped up on pillows, flipping through channels on the TV—Seven's text couldn't have come at a better time.

The apartment feels different now—in a good way. There's a routine emerging, one that revolves around Keely's visits.

Every morning, she comes over to make breakfast. At first, I tried to insist I could manage on my own, but there's something comforting about her presence in my kitchen, the smell of coffee brewing and the sound of her humming softly as she cooks.

We've fallen into an easy rhythm, working together to prepare meals. I may be injured, but I'm not completely useless. I chop vegetables while she mans the stove, our bodies moving in sync in the small space.

During the day, she leaves to help Oakley with inventory or beer bottle recycling at the bar. The hours drag without her, but

I try to keep busy with PT exercises and catching up on game footage. My number one priority is getting back out on the ice.

At night, she brings home dinner, and we settle in to watch an episode of a documentary series we started together. It's become my favorite part of the day - just the two of us, sharing a meal and conversation.

I hear a knock at the door. "Come in!" I call out, knowing it's probably Seven.

The door opens, and Seven pokes his head in. "Ready?"

I nod, reaching for my crutches. "Yeah, just give me a sec."

As I make my way to the door, Seven eyes me carefully. "You sure you're up for this? We don't want to push you too hard."

I appreciate his concern, but I'm determined. "I'm good. Keely's got me on a solid rehab plan. I need to keep moving forward."

Seven nods, a knowing gleam in his eye. "Speaking of Keely... how's that going?"

He steps back and holds my front door open so I can walk out of my apartment on crutches. I shouldn't need these soon. Two weeks is the recommendation, and I'm halfway there, but Keely thinks I'm healing well enough that I can use a cane around the house if I want.

I pause, unsure how to answer. "It's going. She's great at her job."

"Uh-huh," Seven says, not buying it for a second. "And that's all?"

Since when did Seven give a shit about this stuff? He would never have asked about Keely while hinting that he thinks something might be going on.

I sigh, running a hand through my hair. "That's all it can be right now. I need to focus on getting back on the ice."

Technically her words, not mine. But she's right—we both need to focus on our careers for the time being. There's a lot on the line for both of us.

Seven claps me on the shoulder as we head out. "Fair enough. It just looked like something was happening between you two in the bar the night of the accident, and then before I know it, she's your PT and living across the hall."

His words stick with me as we make our way to the gym down the elevator to the underground parking lot of the apartment building. He saw something between us that night too.

But as we enter the gym and I see Brent and Briggs already there, I push thoughts of Keely aside. It's time to focus on getting stronger, on proving to myself and everyone else that I can come back from this.

"Well, look who decided to grace us with his presence!" Brent calls out, a grin on his face.

I roll my eyes, but I can't help smiling. "Missed me that much, huh?"

Briggs laughs and heads in my direction. "The locker room isn't the same without your ugly mug, man."

As the guys settle into their usual workout, the familiar banter starts up. It feels good to be back with the guys, to feel like part of the team again.

I take a seat in the chair that Seven pulled out for me. In one more week, Keely said that I can start adding weights into my routine but until then, I'm just happy to be back with the guys.

"So," Brent says between sets, "how's life with your personal nurse?"

I shoot him a glare. "She's not my nurse, she's my PT. And it's fine."

"Just fine?" Briggs chimes in, glancing over his shoulder while running on the treadmill with Lake to his left. "Come on, man. You're not fooling any of us. We've seen the way you look at her."

"It's not like that. We're just friends," I tell them, though the word 'friends' is almost physically painful to say when referring to Keely.

Seven snorts. "You dropped out of a game of pool to walk her to her car... a winning game."

"You had it under control without me," I say, shrugging it off. "By the way, did we win?"

"No, Romeo, we didn't finish the game. We came running out to find you mangled, laying on the asphalt after we heard tires screech and people outside screaming. We got sidetracked making sure that you were still alive," Lake says, hitting the 'cool down' mode on the treadmill. He must have just finished his cardio for the day.

"And this is one of the two rooms with workout equipment in the building," I hear Sam's voice say as he pushes through the gym doors.

I look over to find a blonde woman, who I'm guessing is about my age, trailing closely behind Sam. She's dressed professionally, and my guess is that she's either involved with a new sponsorship or part of the press. She does seem familiar, but during interviews, it can be hard to know who's who as they all scrunch in together. I just look for a raised hand and point at it anymore.

Sam gives us quick waves as he continues to give her information about the building. She sends us a smile and then they're back out the door in the direction that they came.

"Who's that?" I ask.

Briggs slows down his treadmill, turning it down to 'cool down' as well. "That's Rowan Summers. She's the reporter who's doing the big piece on the Hawkeyes and our comeback year. Sam's giving her full access to the stadium, and she's even going to travel with us for some of our away games."

Brent finishes his last rep and then walks over to his water bottle and takes a big gulp. "Coach Bex hates her."

"Why is that?" I ask.

This is the first I've heard of Rowan Summers or the puff piece. Though Coach Bex not liking reporters isn't news to me. I've heard him attempt to convince Phil Carlton to do away with making us do interviews at the end of every game, but that won't ever happen.

"I don't know. She wrote something about how he's the grumpiest NHL coach who ever lived and how his multi-million-dollar contract should at least buy Phil Carlton a smile once in a while," Brent says.

My eyebrows shoot up at the thought of a reporter going after Coach Bex. "Oh shit..."

"Yep. He's been dodging her all week—it's weird," Briggs says.

Lake hits the kill switch and jumps off the treadmill, finishing for the day. "Yeah, it's like watching that viral video of the hamster chasing the cat that was going around."

Brent's eyebrows scrunch together as he takes another pull off his water bottle. "Wasn't it a mouse and cat?"

"I don't know... either way, Coach Bex trying to avoid a pint-size reporter is unnatural," Lake says.

"Agreed," I chime in.

Thank God I'm back.

Reporter or no reporter, I'm home and being here is the best rehab I could ask for.

And I'll admit, seeing Coach Bex dodge this reporter is a hell of a lot more entertaining than sitting at home.

Chapter Fourteen

Keely

I wave goodbye to the recycling company truck driver as he gets in his truck after he and I loaded all of the beer bottles while my uncle went through the weekly order with the sales rep.

I step inside the bar when I'm done, wiping my hands down with a damp bar towel, the smell of bleach and wood polish mingling in the air. It's just before rush hour— a little later than I've been staying, but Reeve had mentioned he was headed to the Stadium, and the broom closet could use some serious attention.

Turning in the direction of the broom closet, I suddenly bump into someone. My heart races at the unexpected contact. "Oh, excuse me," I say, glancing up to find a familiar pair of dark blue eyes.

"Keely," Dr. Morgan says, the recognition flashing across his face.

My breath hitches for a moment as the memory crashes into me—early mornings in the sterile chaos of the hospital, the urgency of Reeve's situation, and Dr. Morgan, clad in surgical garb. I hadn't expected to ever see him again... but here he is, in the flesh. Now, standing before me, he's transformed into an image of relaxed confidence, sporting soccer shorts and a Tornados jersey that clings to his form.

"Dr. Morgan?" I ask, half-amazed, half-humbled. I can't help but smile, dispelling some of my earlier anxiety.

"Jaxson," he corrects gently, a matching grin making his features even more inviting. "I'm off the clock now. How about you?"

"I just finished the recycling, and now I am going to reorganize the broom closet before I head back to check on Reeve," I say, assuming he is here to discuss his patient.

"How is Reeve doing? I talked to the Hawkeyes doc yesterday, and he said that he seems to be healing nicely," Jaxson says, crossing his arms over his chest and his biceps and forearms flexing when he does.

The sound of approaching footsteps pulls me from their moment, and another familiar voice breaks through our conversation.

"Look at that. Just the man I wanted to introduce you to," my uncle says. "This is Jaxson, the one I told you about who runs the city league team."

"You're Jaxson, the soccer player my uncle wanted me to meet?" I ask.

This city can't be that small, can it?

Jaxson's dark blue eyes and warm smile radiate from him. "I believe so... last time I checked anyway. I was wondering if I'd ever get to meet you outside of the hospital after Reeve's surgery. You weren't here last week."

"Wait, you knew at the hospital that I was Oakley's niece when we met in the ICU waiting room?"

He nods. "Yeah... Well, how many people have the name Keely? And then, when Coach Bex mentioned the cameras outside of Oakley's catching the car, I put it together, but it didn't seem like the appropriate time to bring it up at the hospital. I figured I would catch up with you last week, but you weren't here on Tuesday."

"This is actually one of the first days I've been back at it. I've been working to get Reeve in a good place to start rehab so I haven't been working here much."

He nods in understanding. "So, your uncle says that you used to play soccer?"

"I used to, and then I got injured right before high school. Then college became a full-time job and I just never found the time to jump back in."

"I remember those days in medical school well. It becomes etched in your psyche forever," he says.

"You're right, it does."

We both laugh, and I feel the tension in my shoulders easing. There's something about Jaxson not being in his scrubs and being in serious surgeon mode that makes him almost feel like a different person. But I like it.

Jaxson's eyebrows raise slightly. "I'm here with a group from the team that I captain if you're interested in joining us for a drink?"

I hesitate, tempted by the offer.

"Thanks, but I've got a project to finish up. And I need to grab dinner for Reeve on my way home."

"No problem," he says easily. "But if you ever want to come check out the team, you're more than welcome. We could always use more players—or fans."

"I'll keep that in mind," I reply, surprised to find that I mean it. "Thanks, Jaxson."

As we part ways, I can't help but think that maybe I should give the soccer league a try. It could be fun, a chance to meet new people outside of work.

And if I'm being honest with myself, Dr. Morgan—Jaxson—is even more attractive than I remember from our brief encounter at the hospital. His easy smile and the way his eyes crinkle at the corners when he laughs... I shake my head, pushing the thought aside. I've got enough on my plate without adding complicated feelings to the mix.

As I enter the apartment, the savory aroma of Thai food wafts through the air. Reeve's head pops up from behind the couch and his face lights up at the sight of the takeout bags.

I set them on the coffee table in front of him, but he's already up with one crutch under his arm and heading for the kitchen.

"You're a lifesaver," he calls out over his shoulder. "It smells so good. I'll grab the plates and the forks. Do you want something to drink?"

"You don't need to get it all by yourself. I can help," I tell him.

"You brought the food home, and you've been on your feet all day; I got it."

He's right. I have been on my feet all day, and they are starting to hurt.

"Okay, thanks," I say and then settle onto the couch. I grab the remote and navigate to the documentary we've been watching. "Ready for another episode?"

"Queue it up, I'll be right there," he says.

It's not long before Reeve and I are sitting on the couch together, stuffing our faces and watching a documentary on the most poisonous creatures in the world, and now I'm not sure how I'll sleep tonight without checking my bed for venomous scorpions and centipedes. Which is silly since the Northwest has very little of those kinds of creatures and none of them are even close to as venomous as the ones on the show... I know because I did a quick internet search when Reeve wasn't looking.

Once our show finishes and our to-go containers are all cleared, I bring up the soccer league.

"Dr. Morgan came into the bar today," I say casually.

"He did? To talk to you about me?" he asks.

"No, he's the captain of a soccer city league and told me I should consider joining."

Reeve's eyes light up at the idea. "You should. I think that's a great idea."

"I just haven't played in a while. What if I'm not any good anymore?"

"Come on, Keely," Reeve encourages, nudging my shoulder. "You won't know unless you try. Just go down and check it out next week. What's the harm in that?"

I consider his words, a small smile tugging at my lips. "Maybe you're right. It could be fun to get back into it."

Reeve grins. "See, you're fitting in around here already."

As I head down the hall from Reeve's apartment to mine, I'm already warming to the idea of playing again. Maybe it is time to step out of my comfort zone a little and do something for myself for once.

Chapter Fifteen

Reeve

"That's it, nice and slow," she encourages. "Remember, we're just focusing on flexibility right now. No weight-bearing exercises for that lower body yet."

I nod, gritting my teeth slightly to the pain and discomfort, but no one said that recovery would be easy. "What about my upper body? I feel like I'm losing muscle mass by the day."

Keely considers this. "Actually, that's not a bad idea. We should keep your upper body strength up while we work on your knee."

"The gym at Hawkeyes stadium is always open," I suggest. "We could use that if you want."

Her eyes light up. "That's perfect."

As we finish the stretch, I clear my throat. "There's a home game next week. Sam's clearing me to attend, and the press will probably want to see me there. Would you be interested in coming with me?"

Keely raises an eyebrow. "In your seats?" she asks, a hint of playfulness in her voice.

I chuckle. "Well, I was thinking we'd sit with the fans this time. But next home game, I'll take you up to the owner's box. You can meet Phil Carlton and 'the girls.'"

"The girls?" Keely asks, curiosity piqued.

"The women who run the back office," Reeve explains. "They also happen to be dating most of our starting lineup."

Keely laughs. "Sounds like quite a group. I'd love to meet them."

"Thanks for the ride, man," I tell Brent as he parks in the Hawkeyes parking lot after picking me up.

We're barely through the main entrance when I hear a familiar voice. "Reeve! Hold up a second."

I turn to see Sam jogging towards me, a woman I now know as Rowan Summers trailing behind him.

"I'll meet you in there," Brent says, and I wave as Brent heads for the gym.

"Hey, Sam," I greet him, suddenly feeling a bit self-conscious. "I know you said I could be here now, but if it's a problem—"

Sam chuckles, cutting me off. "No, no, I remember. I'm glad to see you looking better, kid."

I relax a bit, offering a small smile. "Thanks, I'm feeling better too."

That's when I notice Rowan more closely. She's attractive, in a polished sort of way, with a press badge hanging around her neck. Sam catches my curious glance and gestures to her.

"Reeve, this is Rowan Summers. She's a reporter who'll be doing a piece on the Hawkeyes."

Rowan steps forward, extending her hand. "It's nice to meet you, Reeve. I've heard a lot about you."

I shake her hand, noticing the way her eyes light up with interest. "All good things, I hope?" I ask.

Sam interjects before Rowan can respond. "Speaking of which, how are things going with Keely and rehab?"

"Things are good," I reply, my eyes inadvertently shifting to Rowan. She's smiling, hanging on every word as if it's the most fascinating thing she's ever heard. It's a bit unnerving.

Sam nods, seemingly satisfied. "Great to hear. Listen, Reeve, Rowan here will be covering your recovery as part of her story. She'll be at the home games, so if you could spare some time for questions, that'd be great."

I feel a twinge of apprehension but nod anyway. "Sure, I can do that."

Rowan's smile widens. "I promise I'll make it as painless as possible," she says. "But your comeback story will really add some dimension and give readers someone more than just a big franchise to root for. It's more personal."

"Sure, whatever you need," I tell her, but giving away personal information about myself doesn't always come easy to me.

"Thanks, Reeve. I'll see you soon," she says and then turns back to Sam.

As I watch Sam and Rowan walk away, I can't help but wonder what I've just gotten myself into.

When I walk back into the gym, Brent is spotting Lake who's doing squat reps.

"What took you so long, you were right behind me," Brent says.

"Sam caught me and wanted to introduce me to Rowan Summers. I guess part of her piece is going to be on me and my recovery."

"She wants to interview you for the story she's doing on the Hawkeyes?" Brent asks.

"I guess so," I say, moving towards the chair that Seven set up for me last time.

I'd like to jump in and at least work on some upper body work like Keely and I discussed, but I should wait until we can work on it together. I'm anxious to get back into shape, but I'm smart enough to know that I should wait to see what Keely thinks is safe to try.

"Of course she wants Reeve's story. The star player saved a woman in need and suffered a possible career-ending injury. It's a comeback story waiting to happen," Kaenan says.

Lake drops the weights off his shoulders and takes a couple of cleansing breaths.

"And Sam is giving her full access," Lake adds.

"Why does Coach Bex not like her again?" I ask.

I hear the door to the gym close as if someone just walked in.

"Because she sticks her nose where it doesn't belong, and I don't like a snoop," Coach Bex says, his British accent always a little thicker when he's pissed.

He walks into the room, his posture its usual board-straight, his serious facial expression characteristically unreadable. I can count up the times I've seen Coach Bex smile on one finger—once.

"Isn't that literally the job title of a reporter?" Brent snickers.

"That doesn't mean I want her coming around to distract my players with frivolous questions when we should be focused on winning a championship," Coach Bex says, his annoyance for the pint-sized reporter clearly evident. "But she's not your problem and I'm making sure that Sam keeps her out of your hair. If she bothers you too much, come tell me." He turns his attention to the others. "Now, shouldn't you lot be training?"

As the guys scramble back to their workouts, Coach Bex approaches me. His voice lowers, a rare hint of concern breaking through his stern demeanor. "How are you holding up, Reeve? Really?"

"I'm... getting there," I admit. "It's not easy, but I'm working hard with Keely. We're making progress and I can start working out in the gym next week."

Coach Bex nods, his expression unreadable. "Good. The team needs you back, but not at the cost of your long-term health. Don't push too hard, too fast."

His words of caution surprise me, but I appreciate them. "Thanks, Coach. I'll be smart about it."

As Coach Bex moves away to bark orders at the others, I settle into my chair, watching my teammates train. The familiar sounds and smells of the gym wash over me, both comforting and frustrating. I'm itching to join them, but I know patience is key right now.

I pull out my phone, sending a quick text to Keely:

> Reeve: At the gym. What day are you thinking next week that I can start upper body work?

> Keke: A few more days. We'll start slow and work our way up. You're recovering quicker than I expected.

Putting my phone away, I lean back, observing and mentally preparing for the work ahead. The road to recovery is long, but with each passing day, I'm one step closer to getting back on the ice.

Chapter Sixteen

Keely

I watch Reeve carefully as he maneuvers through the narrow row, his crutches clicking against the concrete. The stadium buzzes with energy, but my focus is on him, ready to offer support if needed.

"You good?" I ask, hovering close behind.

"Never better," Reeve grins over his shoulder, though I catch the slight wince as he eases into his seat.

As soon as we're settled, it's like a wave of recognition ripples through the nearby fans. Hands reach out, voices call his name.

"Reeve! Man, it's great to see you back!" One fan says.

"How's the knee, champ? You'll be on the ice again in no time!" Another fan calls out.

Reeve's face lights up, his earlier discomfort forgotten as he basks in the warmth of the crowd. "Thanks. Wouldn't miss this for the world."

I lean in, whispering, "Quite the welcome committee you've got here."

He chuckles, eyes sparkling. "What can I say? Hawkeyes fans are the best."

I begin to understand as I watch him chat animatedly with those around us. This isn't just a stadium; it's a second home. The way Reeve comes alive here, surrounded by the energy and camaraderie – it's a beautiful thing to witness.

"Hey," I nudge him gently. "I think I'm starting to get why you love this place so much."

Reeve's smile softens, and he squeezes my hand. "Just wait till the game starts. Then you'll really see the magic."

The roar of the crowd filled the stadium as Keely settled into her seat next to Reeve. The energy was palpable; fans decked out in Hawkeyes gear, buzzing with excitement for the upcoming game. Just as the announcer's voice booms over the speakers, a slender figure squeezed past them, blonde hair swishing as she took the empty seat on Reeve's other side.

"Rowan," Reeve nods, a hint of wariness in his voice. "Fancy seeing you here."

The woman's bright blue eyes sparkled as she tucked a sleek recorder partially out of view of the fans but visible enough that Reeve and I could both see it. "You know me, always where the story is."

Oh, I see, she's a reporter.

Reeve turns to me, "This is Rowan Summers, she's doing a piece on the team's championship prospects." He then gestured to me, "And this is Keely, my physical therapist."

Rowan's eyes widened with recognition. "You're the one Reeve saved, right? And then became his PT? Talk about a twist of fate!"

Keely shifts uncomfortably. "Yeah, that's about the gist of it."

Leaning in a little closer, Rowan asked, "Any chance there's more going on between you two?"

She catches me off guard and I just about choke on my words.

Reeve intervenes quickly, "The Hawkeyes skating into a championship is a big enough story, don't you think, Ms. Summers?"

Rowan's lips curled into a sly smile. "What can I say? Love or tragedy, every good story needs a hook. That's how we sell out stadiums and jerseys."

"Well, wait four more weeks and you might have your tragedy," Reeve says darkly.

I tense, wanting to protest, but Rowan presses on, "That's not what Sam Roberts says. He thinks you'll be back stronger than ever by Thanksgiving. Thoughts?"

Reeve's jaw set. "All I'll say is it's not over 'til it's over. I'm not ready to retire my jersey just yet."

"Can I quote you on that?" Rowan asks, her recorder inching upward.

"If it's good for the story," Reeve shrugs.

The stadium lights suddenly dim, colorful spotlights dance across the ice. Rowan stands, "I'd better get to the owner's box.

It was a pleasure, Keely – that's K-E-E-L-Y, right? I want to make sure I spell it correctly for the story."

"That's correct," I tell her.

She thanks us both for our time and then as Rowan disappears back up the stairs of the stadium, I blow out a breath. "She's... intense."

Reeve chuckles and reaches over to squeeze my knee. The sensation catches me off guard, but the touch isn't unwanted. "Welcome to the big leagues, Doc. Ready for some hockey?"

Then he turns and sees the look on my face.

"You okay?" he asks, his voice low and concerned.

"Yeah, just... not used to being part of the story," I say.

Reeve chuckles softly. "Welcome to my world. You get used to it, eventually."

Maybe so, but I didn't sign up to get used to it.

After the game, I follow Reeve down to the underbelly of the stadium.

"Come on. I have to do media tonight and I have a group of girls for you to meet."

Girls?

My immediate thought is a group of female fans or scantily dressed puck bunnies. We're not together so I won't allow myself to be jealous. This is his job and he and I aren't together. He's free to do anything or anyone he wants, but it would be easier if I didn't have to see it.

"I'm not so sure I need to meet a bunch of women looking to score with you tonight, they might get the wrong idea about us and think that you're in a relationship. I can wait for you in the lobby," I say.

Reeve's eyebrows downturn at my comment—confusion on his face.

"What? No... not those kinds of girls. The girlfriends of the players I told you about. None of them got to meet you at the bar the night of the accident and they've been bugging me to make an introduction." Oh right. He mentioned that they usually watch the game from the owner's box. "But it's good to know that you get jealous too. I know I should play hard to get, but why should I when I already know what I want."

My heart squeezes at his proclamation, but heart squeezing is the only squeezing we can do from here on out. It's for his own good, or all of this that he loves could go away.

"We talked about this..." I warn, looking around to see if anyone is listening in to our conversation.

"Your issue with us is that you're my PT but you won't always be," he says, leading me further down the hall as I begin to see more and more press badges like Rowan's.

"And when Sam gives me the job?" I ask.

His eyes glance over to mine as we walk side by side. "I won't play hockey forever. I have to retire sometime."

"So, you're planning on what exactly?"

"I plan on running the long game."

"Reeve!" A woman with long dark brown hair comes in, wrapping her arms around Reeve's shoulders and pulling him for a hug. "Oh my God, they told me that you would be available for media tonight but I wasn't sure if Sam finally let you back through the doors."

As soon as she pulls back, I recognize her. Tessa Tomlin—Brent Tomlin's sister and the media manager for the team. I've seen her occasionally on TV when she pops in to answer questions from media when they ask if a player will be interviewing. The social media posts are all curated by her, which sometimes have her in the video shot or her voice making fun interviews with players during practice. It's also common knowledge that she's dating Lake Powers, the Left Wing and captain of the Hawkeyes.

"He only let me back in because he saw it as a good PR move to have me talk to the press," Reeve teases. We all know that Sam cares. He wouldn't have spent all night and early morning in a stuffy hospital waiting room calling specialists and approving Hawkeyes funds for me to take care of Reeve if he didn't.

"You know he loves you. You're like the son he never had," she says "But I'm glad you're back in the stadium. We all missed you."

"I brought someone along with me that you've been begging me to meet," he says, his eyes turning to me.

"Keely! Finally," she says, reaching out with her hands to grab mine. "We saw you two sitting in your seats. The girls are all itching to meet you. Penelope wanted to run down to your row and pull you up to the owner's box to be with us, but we figured you needed to stay with Reeve," then her eyes move back to Reeve. "And holy cow... the fans loved seeing you in those seats. I think the cameraman panned to you two a hundred times. Our social media feed blew up when I posted a short reel, and Lake said it was a huge morale boost for the guys in the locker room to see you back."

"Thanks, Tessa, it's good to be back," he says and then smiles down at me.

"Okay, well, I need to deliver you to media," she says, looking at Reeve, and then turns back to me and squeezes my hands, "And the girls are already waiting over there to meet you," she says.

I nod, "We don't want to keep anyone waiting."

"Okay," she says, dropping my hands and then turns to walk back down the crowded hall. "Follow me."

People pat Reeve's shoulder as we walk by, and he receives smiles from people who are all so happy to see him back.

This is where he belongs, and I will make sure he stays here.

As soon as we get to the room where media is set up for the guys to come in for interviews, Tessa sends Reeve in as Briggs Conley comes out. Reeve gives me one last look before he dips in and my heart flutters because I'm the last thing he looked for before he went in.

Tessa doesn't waste any time as she pulls me down a different hallway but it's not long before I see three women standing together laughing. As soon as we get close, they notice us approaching.

"Look who I found?" Tessa says.

At first glance, I recognized Penelope Roberts.

Her long blonde hair, sweet smile, and the same gray-blue eyes that her father and GM for the Hawkeyes have. Plus, I saw all of her pictures in his office.

"You're Penelope, right?" I ask, reaching out a hand to shake hers. "You got me the interview with your dad and my apartment. I can't tell you how much I appreciate both of those things."

Her smile is bright and inviting as it beams back at me. "No need to thank me, I was just doing my job. I'm glad that Reeve is getting the help that he needs. The reports are that he's doing really well."

"He is. I really think we'll make the deadline for getting him back on the ice," I say and then my eyes move down to the next.

Autumn Daughtry.

She and Briggs Conley were all over social media last year as the "it" couple who weren't supposed to end up together because Briggs is her brother's best friend. And I love how they started a charity that helps young kids with childhood cancer.

"You're Autumn," I say, reaching out a hand to shake hers.

"Yeah," Autumn beams. "It's great to finally meet you. Next time you come to watch a game, let us know and we'll get you a pass for the owner's box."

I nod and then turn to the girlfriend, but then I realize that she's familiar too.

"Hi, I'm Isla," she says, swaying softly, and that's when I realize that she is very pregnant.

"Wait, I know you, don't I? You own Newport Athletics, right? I own like twenty pairs of your leggings," I tell her.

Her face falls just slightly and the rest of the girls eye her quickly. She recovers her smile quickly, though, and nods.

"Yes, I used to, and it's always great to meet people who love the brand. I actually sold off my shares of the company last year and started a new sports line."

"Wow, that's impressive. Congratulations," I say.

Penelope leans in. "And all while juggling a pregnancy and the cutest toddler that you'll ever meet. Isla is a superstar."

"And a toddler?" I ask.

"Berkeley, my three-year-old, is up with her grandmother in the owner's box, probably devouring every cookie in that place."

"We're missing a couple of other girls in our group. Brynn is on a book tour. She's dating Seven Wrenley. His daughter, Cammy, is somewhere around here, but on nights like these, she is always really busy."

I nod. I met Cammy when I came in for an interview with Sam.

Suddenly a warm hand slides across my lower back.

"Hi, Reeve," the women all say in unison.

"Hey, did you all meet Keely?" he asks.

"We did and we already adore her," Autumn says.

"Good," he says and then slides to my side. "I finished with media. Are you ready to go back to the apartment? My leg is getting tired. But you can stay if you want—"

"No, that's fine. I'll head back with you." I say, now realizing that he probably did overdo it, and now I want to make sure he gets ice on it asap.

When I glance back, all four women are watching us intently, smirks on their faces.

"It was nice to meet you all," I say.

They all smile and share the sentiment.

I turn around and start following Reeve back the way that Tessa brought me.

"Hey, Keely?" I hear one of the women say. Reeve and I both turn to glance back at them. "I have a feeling you'll be seeing more of us," Penelope yells and then winks.

When I look back at Reeve, he's already watching me.

Why does Reeve's world have to come with all the bells and whistles?

Chapter Seventeen

Keely

As I approach the city soccer league fields during the after-work hours, the smell of rain from earlier today, freshly cut grass, and the sound of whistles blowing, balls being kicked, and children playing, flood my senses.

The multi-soccer fields are packed with players and spectators who seem eager to start the games.

I scan all the teams across the vast soccer park, each with players in various colored jerseys stretching or warming up, preparing for their matches.

Finally, I spot the field with the familiar Tornados jerseys and notice the metal bleachers off to the side. I head for them, walking to take a seat before the game starts, when a tall figure in blue catches my eye, running straight towards me.

It's Jaxson.

His face breaks into a wide grin as he jogs up to me, his dark blue eyes twinkling. "You made it," he says, slightly out of breath. "I wasn't sure if you'd come."

Honestly, until going to the Hawkeyes home game with Reeve a few days ago and remembering the thrill of being part of a team again, while doing something that you love, I wasn't so sure if I would come either.

I'm glad that Reeve convinced me to come.

"I figured I should check it out," I look around at all the fields. That has to be at least a dozen games all prepping to take place simultaneously. "There's a lot of games going on today."

Jaxson nods, gesturing to the bustling fields around them. "Tuesday nights are always packed. It's great to see so many people out here enjoying the game."

"I can see that," I say, taking in the lively scene.

Jaxson's expression suddenly turns hopeful. "Listen, I hate to put you on the spot, but we're short a player today. One of our guys – his wife just went into labor."

"Oh, whoa..." I say, looking over the team out in front of me and seeing that they are, in fact, short a player.

"And it leaves us in a bit of a bind. Any chance you'd want to jump in? No pressure, of course, but we'd love to have you."

I hesitate, glancing down at my jeans. It's not that I couldn't wear jeans—I've done it before, but it does limit my range of motion more than I'd like and I will stick out like a sore thumb since by the looks of it, everyone else wore athletic shorts. "I'm not exactly dressed for it..."

Jaxson waves my comment off. "Don't worry about that. We've got extra jerseys in the team bag. What do you say? Want to give it a shot?"

I know I can't keep living under a rock. At some point in my life, I'll have to take a chance and put myself out there. If I don't, then someday, I'll wake up without a life at all.

I moved here for a new chance—a new life. How many more times will I say no before I finally say yes? How many more opportunities will I miss out on?

"You know what? Why not? It's been a while since I played, but I'll give it a shot."

Jaxson's face lit up. "Come on, I'll introduce you to the team and we'll get you geared up."

As Jaxson leads me toward the team's bench, the excitement on the field of people getting ready to start the game is contagious. Players in blue Tornados jerseys and the opposing team in orange, are all stretching or passing balls back and forth. There's a mixture of pre-game jitters that you can feel all around, and for once today, it seems that the rain might hold up for the game, though I'm sure everyone would play through it anyway.

"Hey everyone," Jaxson called out, catching the team's attention. "This is Keely. She's going to fill in for Mike tonight. Say, "Hi Keely"."

"Hi Keely," a chorus of welcoming voices greet me as I give a small wave back to everyone. Everyone sends me a warm smile and then quickly gets back to their pre-game regime.

A tall woman with short brown hair steps forward, offering her hand. "I'm Sarah. Welcome aboard, and thanks for jumping in. We would have had to ask Arnold from a few fields over to fill in for us or else we would have had to forfeit... but he's the worst ball hog. No one, including his current team, likes playing with him."

"Thanks," I say, "I'm not a ball hog, but I should warn you that I'm probably a little rusty. I haven't played in a while. I hope I don't let you all down."

"Don't worry about that. We're just here to have some fun. There are a few intense players like Jaxson on the team but I'm sure that you're used to him being like that," she teases, "We're just glad to have a full team. Here, come with me. I have a duffle bag with extra jerseys in it. What do you think you'll fit... a man's extra small?"

I blink for a second, still processing her comment about me being used to Jaxson being like that before I can even think to answer her about my sizing.

"Umm yeah, an extra small is fine, or whatever the smallest jersey you have will work. But what did you mean by me being used to Jaxson being like that?" I ask.

She leads me to a large duffel bag on the sideline and bends down on one knee to rummage through it.

"I just figured that you two are dating?" she says, digging deeper into the bag. "I've never seen him so excited to see someone coming to watch us play. And I've definitely never seen him leave the field to greet anyone before a game. He usually gets in this zone when he gets out on the field, prepping for the game," she says, and then pulls out a blue jersey. "These should fit, yeah? Sorry, I don't have cleats for you."

"It's fine," I say. "So, you know Jaxson well?"

I'm curious about Jaxson a little, and I'm wondering what kind of info she'd be willing to share.

"Yeah, I'd say. I work as a surgical assistant for another surgeon on the same floor. My husband is an anesthesiologist and works with Jaxson in surgery quite a bit."

"Oh, really? Is your husband here playing?" I ask.

She points to the stands where a man is passing out snacks to twin girls. "No, but he shows up to support me and brings our girls out to watch mommy play."

She waves when the twins notice us staring.

Seeing Sarah with her family makes me slightly envious of that kind of support. Besides my uncle, my mom, Paula and a few friends from college that I mostly only keep up with on social media, I don't have someone like that who shows up for me. Someone I can be a team with and share life experiences.

"Well, you have a beautiful family," I tell her.

She smiles over at them. "Thank you. And I'm glad to see Jaxson invited you. It's been a long time since I've seen him date anyone. He's sort of a workaholic, which can come with his line of work, but he's such a good guy. I'd like to see him with a better work/life balance."

"Oh, we're not dating. We met... Well actually, it's a funny story, but basically, my uncle owns Oakley's. He just invited me to come because he knew I'm from out of town," I tell her.

"Really? That's too bad. I was hopeful..."

"I'm sure he doesn't have a difficult time meeting women," I say, trying to cheer her up for some reason.

It's not as if I haven't noticed that Jaxson is good-looking, but I'm still trying to navigate through moving here and my feelings for Reeve. Dating a workaholic doctor who is also Reeve's surgeon sounds complicated. But then again, things between Reeve and I will never change. He and I can't ever date. Not unless he no longer plays a sport professionally.

And I want what Sarah has.

Maybe I need to start putting myself out there more.

I pull off my jacket and pull on the jersey over the t-shirt I have underneath. Sarah gives me an approving nod that the jersey looks good, and then I follow her back out onto the field.

As we rejoin the team, Jaxson's eyes find me again and his eyes sweep down over the jersey I have on.

A soft smile plays on his lips. "Looks good on you. How do you feel?"

Excited, confused, hopeful, anxious... also, wondering if you invited me here for more than because my uncle has been hounding you to get me to play.

"A little nervous but excited. It's been a while since I played. I only came to watch so I wasn't expecting to get thrown into the game."

Jaxson placed a reassuring hand on my shoulder. His touch feels natural—something I wasn't expecting.

"You'll do great. Just have fun out there," he says.

I can feel my nerves kick in, the adrenaline surges and starts to course through my body as I walk onto the field with the team to take our positions. As soon as the referee's whistle pierces through the air, signaling the start of the game, everything else is a blur, and my body takes over like it remembers everything it has to do without me thinking too hard.

It takes a second to find my rhythm with the team, but over the next hour, I lose myself in the match – the thud of the ball, the shouts of the players around me, the rush of sprinting down the field. But most of all... I lose myself in being a part of a team again.

By the time the final whistle blows, I'm breathless and exhilarated. The Tornados won 3-2, with me managing to assist on one of the goals. Jaxson catches my eye as the team gathers to shake hands with our opponents and grins.

"So, what did you think? Ready to join the league for real?"

I laugh, wiping sweat from my brow. "You know what? I just might be."

Chapter Eighteen

Reeve

It feels fucking good to be back sitting in the player's box, even though I'm still sidelined.

And walking back into the stadium without crutches like I had the last time I was here feels like a small victory, though the brace around my knee is still a reminder to everyone I see that I'm not here to play

The cool air from the ice sends a familiar chill down my throat and nips at any exposed skin as I watch my teammates glide across the rink. The rhythmic scraping of blades on ice fills my ears, and the sharp crack of sticks hitting pucks as my feet itch to get into the action.

I close my eyes for a moment, inhaling the crisp scent of the freshly cleaned ice in the stadium that I've called home for the last three years and that I hope to continue playing in for years to come. A sense of relief hits when I hear Coach Bex's whistle screech to stop a play that the team is practicing through.

I'm here.

I still have a shot at coming back.

They could have benched me—they could have traded me—but they still see the potential in me that I know I still have. In only a few more weeks, I'll prove I'm ready to get back out on the ice.

I hear a ding on my phone as a text comes through from Keely.

A smile tugs at my lips at her name across my phone.

She left this morning to do inventory at Oakley's after we made breakfast together and worked through my stretches. I'm more sore than usual, but I told her I wanted to kick things up a notch. I can handle the pain of rehab. What I can't handle is not making it to my self-imposed goal.

> Keke: Taking your advice. Heading to soccer practice after inventory at Oakley's. Wish me luck!

My thumbs hover over the keyboard, quickly typing up a reply.

I'm happy to see her deciding to go for it and get back out there. And maybe there's a swell of pride in my chest that she credits me for giving her the advice she needs to take the plunge finally.

We're good for each other. I wish she'd see that, but she has to do what's right for her and I'd never push her into anything more. She has to come to her own conclusions about us.

> Reeve: That's great, Keely! You've got this. Show them what you're made of.

Then a feeling comes over me that maybe she needs a little more reinforcement if it took me encouraging her to get out there.

> Reeve: I'm proud of you for doing this.

My phone buzzes again.

Keke: Thanks, Reeve. I'll let you know how it goes.

> Reeve: Looking forward to hearing all about it. Kick some grass out there, Doc.

I can already imagine her eye roll when I see that she read the message, and I audibly laugh to myself.

Keke: Wow, that was terrible. Stick to hockey, Aisa.

> Reeve: I've got a million of them. I'll tell you all of them tonight over dinner. Good luck out there, superstar.

The sound of Coach Bex's whistle blows again and pulls me from Keely and our texts. The team skates over almost lazily as if a little annoyed at Coach Bex's redirection, but he's the best at what he does and we're a better team for having him, though it's easy to say that on sitting on the bench than having a whistle blown at you every few seconds.

I get it.

I shake my head at the thought of actually missing being barked at my Coach Bex. Perspective is a funny thing, and right now I'm getting more of it than I can handle.

And right down the street, Keely's taking steps forward, and I'm glad that I get to be a part of that journey, even if it's just from the sidelines.

The team runs the play again and nails it this time.

A loud clapping sounds beside me.

I got so lost in thought and practice that I didn't notice Sam coming up to stand next to me.

"How are you feeling?" he asked, taking a seat next to me.

I turn to see him in his black Hawkeyes shell jacket.

"Better every day. I think I'm going to make my deadline happen."

Sam's brow furrowed slightly. "Don't overdo it, Reeve. The last thing we want is for you to re-injure yourself. Come back when you're truly ready."

I nod, knowing Sam's right but we wouldn't be athletes playing at this level of the game, earning the size paychecks we get if we didn't push ourselves past the norm to get here.

Let's be honest, Phil Carlson doesn't pay millions for my contract, for me to pussyfoot around.

As Sam walks away, Rowan appears and slides into the seat next to me, taking Sam's spot. "Got time for a few more questions?" she asked with a smile.

"Sure," I say. "What do you want to know?"

"Tell me about your history as a hockey player. When did you first fall in love with the sport?"

Damn, that's a long history lesson. But we'll start with the basics.

"I've been skating since before I could walk. But I really fell in love with hockey in Alaska. Then when my mom died and I moved to Texas my sophomore year. It's no exaggeration that hockey saved me."

Rowan's expression softened. " I think I do remember hearing about your mother in old interviews you've had. You were young when it happened, right? Would you mind telling me more about—"

"I'd rather not discuss that," I cut in. " She was an amazing person who believed in my dreams of making it to a hockey championship. Let's keep things on the lighter side. I'm partial to puff pieces myself," I add with a smile.

Rowan nods, respecting his boundaries Though I think I saw her wince when I said "puff pieces."

"Then the championship win this year must mean a lot to you. Would it be farfetched for readers to assume that you're dedicating this year's win to your mother?"

"You could say that."

The memories of my mother aren't what I expected to discuss today when I came down to watch practice. I'm about done discussing them right now.

"Would you say that you believe she's watching down on you?"

She's leading me into the quote she wants in order to spice up her piece but I'm not the puppet for that job and I don't like the idea of her fishing around about information pertaining to my mom.

She'll need to find someone else for her shock and awe. My mother and her struggles won't be splashed around headlines for people to see. She might be long gone now, but I'll still protect her memory. No reporter is going to exploit her pain, or mine, for page reads.

"You're trespassing now, Summers. Get back behind the gate," I tell her, letting know that there are some bits of me I've never let her access.

"Of course, sorry. Occupational hazard. Don't release the dogs on me," she says, her reporter-hungry eyes softening.

"You're in luck, I don't have any dogs."

"Really?" she says. "How about Coach Bex?"

Her eyes turn out to the ice, finding the Coach standing in the middle of the rink going over a new play with the team.

"He's nothing more than a Chihuahua. Yappy bark, tiny bite."

I actually don't mean it. It sounded too funny not to say. Coach Bex has no bark—just bite... and he'll swallow you whole.

"Can I quote you on that?"

"If you have a death wish..." I warn teasingly.

Because if she puts that out, she and I both will be swimming with the fishes.

"He's not easy to work with, is he?" she asks, an annoyance in her voice, like she already knows the answer.

"He's not that bad really. He's stuck his neck out for me more times than I can count. But if he thinks that you pose any threat to the team, the players, Sam or Phil... he'll go for your jugular," I nod, staring out at the man who helped pull me off the asphalt that night and helped the EMT load me into the ambulance. And if I wasn't mistaken, I think I saw his eyes well right before they closed the ambulance doors.

" I believe you. Because I've seen the "going for the jugular" first hand," she says.

"Now that I think about it, he's more like a T-Rex," I tell her, pulling my elbows to mimic a short arm. "He looks terrifying, but in truth, the poor guy is just pissed that he has short arms."

She breaks out in laughter as I wave my shorts T-Rex arms around.

"Oh God..." she says, wiping a tear from her eye. "Please don't tell him I laughed at that. I have a hard enough time with him as it is."

"Are you kidding? I'd get a bench for a whole season."

We share a quick smile and then she looks back at her notes.

"Okay, fine. Tell me more about your time in Alaska then..."

Now we're getting somewhere good.

I spend the next twenty minutes telling her about all the trouble I got in as a kid. Alaska was as cool of a place to grow up as I could ever imagine, and someday, I hope to move back and raise a family there.

There's some pain in the memories of where I grew up... but love still lives there too.

After practice, I head back to the apartment and spend the afternoon at home.

My phone buzzes with a call from Seven.

"Hey what's up?" I answer.

"Want to head down to shoot some pool at Oakley's. Brynn says I'm distracting her while she tries to write."

Seven being a distraction seems unlike him.

He barely talks unless you're one-on-one with him.

"What are you doing that is so distracting?" I ask.

"Laying naked on the day bed in her office."

"Get him out of here!" I hear Brynn's voice in the background. "I have a deadline. Please, Reeve."

I can't hold back my snicker at the mental picture of Seven lying naked on the tiny twin-sized day bed in Brynn's apartment across the street.

"Put on some pants. Make your girlfriend happy," I say.

He grunts in annoyance at me siding with Brynn.

I wouldn't want that hairy man butt-ass naked on my couch, either.

"That's the opposite of what should make her happy," Seven argues. "Besides, she's writing one of those sexy scenes right now... I was trying to be helpful with market research."

"Reeve, I'll pay you anything you want!"

"Brynn, I spend hours on this body for you to enjoy. And should I remind you about Cancun? It worked like a charm last time."

"Oh god...." I hear the annoyance in her voice and the clicking of the keys on her keyboard.

"I'll meet you downstairs," I tell Seven.

"I owe you!" Brynn says.

I send a text to Keely to let her know where I'll be in case she shows up with dinner and doesn't know where I am.

> Reeve: Headed to the bar with Seven for a bit. See you later.

It doesn't take long before Seven and I find an open table and rack up the balls.

"Reeve," I hear Oakley before I see him.

He sets a heavy box of long-neck IPA on the bar top and then heads toward up.

"Hey, Oakley," I say, and Seven gives him a nod.

"You boys coming down to play some pool?" he asks, watching Seven select a pool stick.

"Yeah, Brynn called, begging me to get Seven out of her hair."

"Hey..." I hear Seven warn. "What gives man... calling me out like that?"

Oakley and both smirk.

"Do you have a minute?" Oakley asks. "I'll just take a second."

"Sure," I say.

"I'll head to the bar and get us drinks—rootbeer for you?" Seven asks, knowing that I don't like to drink during the season until it's to celebrate a win.

"Yeah, thanks,"

"Hey Aaron," Oakley calls over his shoulder to the bartender. "Reeve and Seven drink free today. And Reeve... from here on out."

I glance over at Aaron, who simply nods to Oakley's instruction, and then I shoot a look at Seven, who just shrugs back at me—neither of us is sure what's going on.

Oakley usually comps all the player's first two drinks on the house during home games since we bring in so much business, not that any of us ever ask or want to take advantage. He says it's just good business. But Oakley treats us well even if he didn't comp our drinks so we'd keep coming back either way.

"You don't have to—"

"Here, follow me," he says.

I turn to follow him, walking to the back of the house toward the inventory room. The door to the room is open as we pass by. Stacked boxes with long necks and canned beer will likely all get sold by this weekend's game even though the team will be away.

He stops at the end of the hall that leads to the bathrooms, but with only a handful of us in the bar, since happy hour hasn't started, we won't be bothered.

"Listen, Reeve. I wanted to thank you properly for what you did for Keely."

I can't hide the look of surprise on my face. He doesn't need to thank me for what happened with Keely.

Maybe that's because she feels like mine to protect, but I won't tell him that because she's not mine.

"You don't need to thank me, Oakley. I just did what anyone would do."

"Not anyone," Oakley says, shaking his head. "You put yourself in harm's way to protect her. That means something to me." He pauses, his eyes growing distant. "Keely... She means everything to me. After her father went away, I promised myself I'd always look out for her."

Her father went away?

I want to ask him exactly what that means, but that feels like a conversation I should have with her.

I nod and lick my lips instead. "She's lucky to have you in her corner."

Oakley's gaze sharpens on me. "And now she has you too, it seems."

"She'll always have me," I blurt out.

His eyes focus on me for a second long. "Hmmm... I had a feeling." he says to himself.

"What does that mean?" I ask, but Oakley doesn't answer.

He turns and heads back down the hallway, calling out over my shoulder. "It means drinks are on me.

Walking out of the hallway, more confused than when I entered, I get a text from Keely.

> Keke: Jaxson invited me to the bar with the soccer team. We won our game!

A small endorphin rush kicks in at the thought of seeing Keely in a matter of minutes.

She's on her way here and she won her game, a surge of pride fills me and I want to celebrate with her but letting her have this moment is important. She says that she needs to settle her home before she can think about a relationship with anyone and this a step in that direction for her to make friends and build a life that will make her want to stay.

About 30 minutes later, Keely walked in with her new teammates.

My eyes find her in the crowd immediately.

Her new blue jersey— her hair pulled back in a messy ponytail—cheeks still flushed from the game—a wide smile across her lips, and she chats with a couple of women from the group as they wait by the bar to order their drinks.

"Hey," I call out, heading straight for her. "Congratulations on the win."

Keely beams over at me as I head for her at the bar.

My breath hitches when she looks at me with so much happiness in her eyes.

"Thanks!" she says, wrapping her arms up over my neck. I want to pull her closer—Squeeze her tighter, but there will be another time....I hope. "It felt amazing to be back on the field."

"I'd like to come to one of your games sometime if you tell me when it is," I say. "A jersey looks good on you."

Though I wish you were wearing mine.

Her jersey is a spare without a number or a last name on it like everyone else's. And I wonder if one day she'll finally let me put AISA on the back.

"Really?" she asks, her eyes glimmering back at me.

"I'll wear your number with 'Woods' on the back, too," I say.

She rolls her eyes playfully as if I'm messing with her.

"Trading in your Aisa jersey already, Mr. Woods? That might look pretty good on you," she teases.

I lean in a little closer—blocking out the noise between us and all other distractions—my vision locking with hers—I'm close enough to feel his breath against my lips.

"Just show me where to sign on the marriage certificate."

Keely laughs, making my heart skip a beat but that wasn't a joke.

"You like to run before you walk, don't you," she said softly.

"Race you to the courthouse?" I ask because, damn it, it's worth a try.

"Reeve," I hear a booming voice call out.

I look to our left as Dr. Morgan heads straight for us, and the way his eyes cut from me down to the woman I practically just proposed a quickie wedding to has my hands clenching at my side—not a usual reaction from me. I don't think I've ever felt jealous before.

Not until Keely.

His eyes return to me as he squares up, but now, he is focusing on me instead of Keely, like he's back in doctor mode. "You're looking good. How does that knee feel? Is the brace giving you enough support?"

"It feels good. Keely's been doing a good job. I think I'll be back on the ice in a couple of weeks."

Even though you thought my career was over.

But I don't tell him that. I know well enough that doctors can only give you their best guess. They don't hold crystal balls. And recovery is up to the individual. If I had gotten the surgery and sat on the couch for months, then I probably wouldn't have a shot. And technically, it's too early to know for sure.

"She's a good PT, I have no doubt," he says, giving her a brief smile. "Let me know how it goes. I'd like to see you back on the ice and I think I have you on the schedule to go over your scans in a month, right?"

"Here, Keely. The bartender said that this was your drink." One of her female teammates says, handing her a hard apple cider.

"Thanks," she tells her.

She takes a sip and then I turn back to Dr. Morgan.

"Yeah, that's right," I say. "I'm hoping to get cleared in two weeks for practice."

Though the Hawkeyes doctor will clear me for practice, Coach Bex wants a second opinion from Dr. Morgan before I play a game.

"That's only six weeks after surgery."

There's a surprised expression on his face.

"I'll be ready."

He nods. "Okay, it's your call," he says, and then looks down at Keely. "The team has a table. You ready?"

"Oh... sure," she says, and then glances over at me. "I'll see you later?"

He places a hand gently at the back of her arm and then escorts her to a table in the back corner.

I head back to Seven. He hands me the pool cue that I usually use and I grip it a little tighter than I should. I bend down to take my shot, trying to focus on the game, but my eyes keep drifting back to Keely, laughing and celebrating with her new team.

I'm happy that she has a team to play with, but the doctor's arm draped over the back of her chair—that I don't like.

Seven noticed my distraction. "You okay, man?" he asked quietly.

I nod, forcing myself to look away from Keely. "Yeah, I'm fine," I say, then line up my shot. "Let's play."

Chapter Nineteen

Keely

The familiar hum of conversation and clinking glasses fills Oakley's as I process payments for bar tabs.

With Reeve getting cleared to travel with the team this week, I find my eyes darting to the TV screen more often than I mean to at the Hawkeyes game.

He looked as excited as a kid packing for summer camp when I brought over dinner a few nights ago. I sat on his bed while we ate Chinese food, and he told me about the lineup of teams they would play and the level of difficulty he felt that the team would have with each game.

It was like having my very own sports channel broadcaster giving the rundown, and I hung on every word. Maybe someday—hopefully a long time from now, Reeve could be a sports reporter when he retires from playing. Though I think he would be a great coach too. I think Reeve can pretty much do anything he wants to.

There's been a void around the apartment for the last couple of days since he's been gone, so when the cameraman flashes over to Reeve sitting in the seats with Hawkeyes fans who came to the away game, my eyes lock on, and I forget what I'm doing. It's been five weeks today since the accident, and next week, we will find out if the Hawkeyes doctor will clear him to play.

"Earth to Keely!" Penelope's voice cuts through my thoughts. "The card reader has been beeping at you for a solid minute."

I blink away my stare and then stare down at the black card reader with its red light flashing at me, "Remove the card for the reader"... oops. "Sorry. I guess I zoned out."

Autumn leans in, her voice lowered to avoid anyone but the girls around her to hear. "Thinking about a certain injured goalie?"

"I'm just worried about his recovery," I deflect and then run the next card stacked by me.

Tessa snorts. "Sure, that's all it is."

Before I can respond, a newcomer saddles up to the bar next to them with a huff as she flops down on a bar stool.

"You're here!" Penelope says, sitting too close and pulling the woman with short brown hair in against her for a side hug.

"Thank God that Seven is out of town this week. I love the man but he thinks every chapter I write needs 'inspiration'. I swear he thinks that my apartment is a nudist colony. I can't get him to put on any clothes," she huffs. "I love him, and the sex is incredible, but if he doesn't let me finish this book, I'm calling HR for sexual harassment."

"You can't call HR. He's doing *pro-boner* work," Tessa teases, and all the girls bust up laughing.

"Just do what I do and tell him that "good boys get treats." Autumn says. "I don't withhold sex because that hurts us both, but if Briggs wants a surprise, he has to check something off the honey-do list."

"What's the surprise?" Brynn asks.

"I purchase something online. It can be really simple—nothing crazy. Like, last month, he opened a package that came in from the mail while I was in Walla Walla visiting our parents and he opened it. It's a new fancy spatula for large cookies, but... that's not what he thought it was for," Autumn says, wiggling her eyebrows.

"Oh my God, what happened?" Tessa asks.

"I came home to the entire house clean from top to bottom, and the new shower head I ordered was put in our master bathroom."

The girls all laugh again.

The door to Oakley's opens, and I give a casual, quick glance, a force of habit. We have to keep track of our body count inside the building to keep off the fire department's shit list. They're always nice enough, but it's better if we can avoid someone calling us in for the violation.

My eyes flash back to the door when I realize who just walked in—Jaxson.

He takes a quick look around in search of someone. His easy smile lights up his face as he spots me.

The more time I spend around him, the more I can see why women left balloons and flower arrangements by his office door.

He weaves through the crowd, heading straight for me, not taking his eyes off me for a second. His dark blue scrubs with a black puffy Patagonia jacket over the top

I can't help but notice the women and a few men who rubberneck when he walks by, and I get why. He's gorgeous—tall and broad—a great soccer player and seems to be a really good guy if my gauge of him is accurate.

"Keely," he says, leaning against the bar. "This place is packed. I've never been here except during happy hour."

"Oh really? Surgeons don't get days off?" I tease, remembering what Sarah said, that he doesn't take much time off.

Aaron hands a fan a drink he ordered, and then he moves past Jaxson, giving Jaxson a spot to lean up against the bar.

"I don't take too many nights off, but I was going over case notes and needed to walk to clear my head. I figured you might be here."

The girls sitting nearby go quiet, and I can feel their gaze on us. I glance quickly at them to find that they all are sporting frowns.

A moment later, a fan walks up behind them and asks if she can get a picture with the 'girls of the Hawkeyes.' They smile, and all agree, giving Jaxson and me some privacy.

The fan's request reminds me that my father's transgressions could blow up at any time, causing not only an issue for Reeve's career but everyone else in the Hawkeyes' family. Could I live with myself if I did that to them?

Jaxson leans in closer across the bar. He smells clean, like mint with just a hint of coffee. I can already see him in his office late at night in the hospital, going on patient files, chewing gum to stay awake, and sipping on stale coffee from the last batch that the reception staff made on his floor before going home.

There's something sexy about a surgeon who cares about his work and the lives he's changing.

"Listen, Keely. There's a real reason for why I came down here. I was wondering if you'd like to grab dinner sometime."

My heart thumps against my chest at his request.

Dinner... he wants dinner.

"He's no Reeve." my brain objects.

And then, my peripheral vision, snags on the four women smiling and taking pictures with happy fans.

I don't get to have Reeve, that's a cruel truth. Not if I care about all these people in his life who are now in mine.

Jaxson is undeniably attractive, kind, and successful. If Reeve weren't in the picture, I would have already agreed, looking forward to calling Paula and telling her that Seattle is already looking up.

Then the sound of people on TV going wild, and the flashing light at the stadium cause me to glance over at the TV.

Reeve's on the screen again, sitting with the fans, wearing some hilarious homemade foam hat that a fan must have lent him.

My heart warms as I watch him on TV and then he turns around with the cameras at his back.

A piece of duct tape covers his last name and written over it in chunky black marker he wrote Mr. Woods on the back.

My belly flips and I bite down on the inside of my lip to keep my smile from growing too large.

The bar starts to laugh as people see it.

He's so happy to be with the team and to be with the fans.

This is his happy place, and I care about him too much for him to carry the burden that my father set on my shoulders. Someday, if he ever finds out he'll thank me for this.

When I look back to Jaxson, who just witnessed Reeves's stunt. He looks at me in question, and then I know my answer.

"I'd love to," I say. "But can you wait? I promised myself that I would finish Reeve's rehab before I dated anyone."

He nods. "I understand. The patient comes first."

"He meets with Hawkeyes doctor next Thursday, how about after that?"

Jaxson's warm smile goes a long way to make me feel like I'm doing the right thing.

"I have Sunday night off. Does that work?"

I nod, and then I notice Sarah's husband, the anesthesiologist in full Hawkeyes' gear as he walks up and pats Jaxson on the back. "Who let you out of the hospital? Come have a beer with me," he tells Jaxson.

Jaxson turns to look back at me, searching for his answer.

I nod. "It's a date."

It's just after midnight when my uncle tells me I can head back to the apartment, but he makes me wait for him to walk out to my car.

The fans have dwindled, but after the girls left an hour ago, I went to the back to jump on inventory since the next game is supposed to be busier because it will be the weekend.

I grab my jacket and my purse to head out when I see my uncle still processing card payments.

"Just a second, Keely. I just have a couple to finish and then I'll walk you."

"I can do it," I hear Jaxson's voice.

I turn to find that he's still in the bar.

"You're still here? I thought you left?" I ask, pleasantly surprised to see him.

Jaxson tucks his hands in the pockets of his jacket.

"You looked busy with the crowd earlier. I didn't want to get in the way. And it turned out that a few guys from the surgery department were here to watch the game so I stuck around. If you're headed out, I'll walk with you."

"That would be great, thanks." I turn to my uncle who I just now realize is watching us with a steady eye. "Jaxson is going to take me so you don't have to leave Aaron and ——."

"Okay," he says, with a weary tone.

It catches me off guard since he seemed to be a big fan of Jaxson. Or at least a big fan of Jaxson getting me back out on the field.

"I'll text you when I get back to my apartment," I tell my uncle over my shoulder as I round the bar, pulling my own jacket on.

It's a newer puffy down jacket that I bought after realizing that the coat I brought with me from Arizona wasn't going to keep me warm this winter in Washington, and I can't expect Reeve to be around to give me his hoodie every time it's pouring down rain.

Jaxson leads me out of the bar and soon, the cool Seattle night air nips at my cheeks as we walk along the sidewalk, headed for my car. The street is quiet, with only a few people hurrying by, collars turned up against the chill. It's a clear night tonight, the moon casting a soft glow on the wet pavement, reflecting in puddles left by an earlier rain.

"So, how are you liking Seattle so far?" Jaxson asks, his breath visible in the cold air.

I hug my new jacket closer, grateful for its warmth. Is it weird that I resent it for not smelling like Reeve? Instead, it still has that department store smell mixed with a little bit of me.

"It's different from Arizona, that's for sure. But I'm starting to feel at home here. Did you grow up in Seattle?"

"I actually grew up in Sacramento, California," Jaxson replied. "But I've been in Seattle for about ten years now, since medical school. It feels like home."

He's been out of school for ten years so that makes him four to five years older than me.

"I can see why. There's something charming about it, even with all the rain."

Jaxson chuckles. "Give it some time, and you'll get used to the rain."

As we approach the crosswalk, Jaxson instinctively places a gentle hand on the back of my arm. We wait for the WALK sign to illuminate, and then Jaxson and I look both ways before we start across the street.

The memory of being in this crosswalk with Reeve flashes through my mind every time I walk through it.

We get to the other side safely and start walking through the parking lot toward my car.

"So... becoming a doctor. When did you decide to take on a mountain of school debt and pick a career where you work a million hours," I ask.

He takes a deep breath and then exhales, the heat of his mouth blowing out billows of steam. "When I was young, I thought I'd become a professional soccer player. Or, more accurately, my father wanted me to be a professional soccer player. I received a full-ride scholarship to play soccer, and I thought I was on the path I was meant to be on. Then, one fateful night changed everything. I couldn't even look at a soccer ball for years."

"What happened?"

"Let's just say that soccer did me dirty and I didn't want anything to do with it. The next day my mom found out that my dad gambled away our house, and she divorced him. I decided I wanted to do something good for others and being a doctor seemed to fit the bill."

I'm taken aback by how similar our stories are. Both of our fathers are the worst, and we both went into the medical field to help others. Mine might have been to clear my father's karma that seems to keep following me around, but also because Paula gave me a new passion when one dream I thought had died with my injury.

Jaxson also suffered a traumatic event and it pushed him into medicine and making a difference. Maybe Jaxson and I are more compatible than I thought. Maybe he's not just the alternate choice from Reeve? What if he turns out to be the better choice?

The soft glow of my phone illuminates while I lay on my bed.

Reeve's name comes over my phone, and my lips pull into a wide, dopey grin the second I see it.

"Hey, how's the road trip going?" I ask casually, trying not to let him know how happy I am that he's calling.

"It's alright. The guys are in rare form tonight. I think Briggs is trying to convince the rookies that he once wrestled a bear in Alaska, but it's more like he got in a slapping match with the Bears hockey team mascot... while we played them *in* Alaska."

I laugh, picturing the scene of Briggs having it out with a plush mascot. With all that padded fur, it must have been more of a pillow fight.

"And how are you doing? Have you been keeping up with your stretches?"

"Yes, doc." There's a hint of playful exasperation in his tone. "I've been a good patient, I promise. How about you? How was Oakley's tonight?"

I hesitate for a second, not completely sure if I should tell him about the date with Jaxson. Instead, I remember the moment on TV that I caught. "It was... interesting. The girls all came in, and I finally got to meet Brynn. The girls all gave her some interesting advice."

"Oh yeah? What kind of advice?"

I consider telling him about the honey-do list and the spatula but decide against it. Girl talk is meant for girls. Reeve doesn't need to hear it.

"Never mind about that actually, you'd find it boring," *Yeah right, not a chance.* "I saw your stunt tonight with the jersey."

I can practically hear his toothy grin over the phone. "Oh yeah? You saw that?"

"I did." I bite down on my lip, then decide to push forward with what I need to tell him. "Actually, something else happened tonight. Dr. Morgan came into the bar."

The silence on the other end of the line stretched for a moment.

"Jaxson was there?" Reeve's voice comes in quiet.

"Yeah," I say. "He, um... he asked me out on a date."

More heavy silence falls between us, thick with unspoken words. Finally, he speaks again. "Oh? And what did you say?"

My heart races and my stomach swirls uncomfortably. "I told him I'm not in a good place to date right now. That I need to finish what I started with your recovery first."

I hear the sound of Reeve blowing out a heavy breath and my heart sinks but this is the right thing for him... for both of us. We can't be together, so inevitably, one of us has to move on first. And with him wearing a jersey with Mr. Woods on the back in front of thousands of fans and even more television viewers... I think I have to be the first one.

"I see," he said, his voice softer now. "Keely, you know you don't owe me anything, right? If you want to go out with Jaxson, you should."

He always tries to make everything easy on me, never letting me feel guilty for anything. Maybe that's Reeve Aisa's most toxic trait, making himself too damn easy to love.

"I know. But it's not just about owing you. I... I need to focus on this. On helping you get back on the ice. It's important to me."

There's another small pause and then he speaks.

"Thank you, Keely. That means a lot to me," his voice is warm this time. "I'll see you when I get home. Don't watch any episodes of that new docu-series without me."

I smile to myself.

At least after all this is over, maybe he and I can at least be friends.

I want to keep Reeve in my life because he's the best friend I've ever had.

Chapter Twenty

Reeve

Sitting on the padded table in the belly of the stadium, running through every strength and stress test on my knee that Dr. Omar could do, I wait with bated breath to hear his prognosis.

We still have a week and a half before he assesses me at my six-week appointment, but I'm hoping that this appointment will give me a glimpse into what I can expect for an answer as to whether he's going to clear me for practice or not.

I glance over at Coach Bex who's standing in the corner of the exam room, one arm crossed over his chest, his other elbow perched against it with his hand resting against his mouth.

He's as anxious as I am to get the news.

Finally, Dr. Omar looked up from my knee after rotating my leg—the last test, he told us he wanted to run. He jots down some notes on his clipboard, a hint of a smile playing at the corners of his mouth. "Well, Reeve, I have to say I'm impressed. Your knee is looking remarkably good, especially considering the severity of the initial injury."

There's an audible exhale from both Coach Bex and myself.

I feel a surge of hope, but I try to keep my expression neutral. "That's great to hear, Doc. So what does that mean for my recovery timeline?"

Dr. Omar glances at Coach Bex before answering. "Honestly, I'm tempted to clear you now. Your range of motion is excellent, and the strength tests are promising. Your PT did an excellent job, and your body seems to be healing nicely. However," he holds up a hand, sensing my excitement, "I want to wait for one more set of scans before I let you skate out for practice. We can't afford to rush this and risk re-injury."

Coach Bex steps forward, his arms crossed. "And when will those scans be ready?"

"By the end of next week," Dr. Omar replies. "If they look as good as I expect them to, we could be looking at clearance for light practice at the six-week mark, assuming that Dr. Woods agrees. And I want Dr. Morgan to take a look, too, before you're cleared for more than that."

My heart races at the prospect of making the deadline that I set. Getting cleared for practice is better than nothing, but every game I miss feels like an eternity. If I want to get back out there and help my team make it to the playoffs, I need to be able to play.

Coach Bex nods, his expression softening slightly. "That's good news, mate. But remember, we need you at 100%. No cutting corners, understood?"

"Yes, Coach," I say. "I'll do whatever it takes."

As we wrap up the appointment, I glance at the clock on the wall and realize with a start that I've completely lost track of time. Keely's soccer game – I promised I'd be there.

"I hate to rush out," I say, hopping off the table, "but I've got somewhere I need to be. Thanks, Doc. Coach, I'll see you at practice tomorrow?"

Coach Bex nods, a knowing look in his eye. "Off you go then. Don't keep her waiting."

I feel a flush creep up my neck, but I don't deny it. As I hurry out of the stadium and to my car, my mind races with possibilities. The future I've been working towards is within reach – both on and off the ice. Now I just have to make sure I don't mess it up.

Pulling into the emptying parking lot, I notice players and spectators loading into their cars and getting ready to leave.

My stomach sinks—I missed it.

She knew I had a late doctor's appointment when I told her I was coming to her game today. And I told her I'd be cutting it close but now I've missed it entirely.

As I approach the tightly cut green grass, the late afternoon sun is starting to set across the soccer fields. The last few players toss their duffel bags over their shoulders and head in the opposite direction, waving at me as they go. My eyes scan the crowd, searching for Keely.

The moment I spot her, I see she's talking with Dr. Morgan near the sidelines, her cheeks flushed from exertion and her hair pulled back in a messy ponytail. She looks beautiful.

But I'm not the only one who notices.

Jaxson stands close. Closer to Keely than I'd like. He smiles down at her. I'll admit the guy is in good shape for someone who spends most of his waking hours working in a hospital. And he's not only good at his job, he's one of the best in his field. I don't have to wonder why Keely agreed to dinner.

And the biggest kicker?

He's not Keely's patient.

I hesitate for a moment, not wanting to interrupt. But then Keely glances up and sees me. Her face breaks into a wide smile, and she waves me over.

"Reeve, you made it!" she calls out.

I jog the last few steps to join them, my knee feeling strong and capable under me. "Hey, sorry I'm late. How'd the game go?"

"We won." Keely beams. "It was close, but we pulled it off in the end."

Jaxson nods in agreement. "Keely here scored the winning goal. She's been a great addition to the team."

I feel a twinge of... something. Pride? Jealousy? I push it aside and focus on congratulating Keely.

"That's awesome! I wish I could have seen it."

Dr. Morgan glances at his watch. "I've got to run - emergency surgery. Great game, Keely. See you next week." He nods to me. "Reeve."

As he walks away, I turn to Keely "So, things are going good with the doctor?" I ask.

"We're not together. I told you... I'm not going on a date with him until after your six-week check-up."

"Right. Okay," I say, because what else is there to say?

She won't consider us since I'm her patient, and with the way things are going, she'll be the new PT for the Hawkeyes.

"Oh! You had your appointment today," she says, her eyes sparkling with excitement. "So? How did it go?"

I can't help but grin. "Really well, actually. The doctor says I'm healing faster than expected. If I keep up with my PT, I might be back on the ice in a few weeks."

Keely's face lights up. "Reeve, that's incredible. I'm so happy for you."

Without thinking, I pull her into a hug. She stiffens for a moment, then relaxes into my embrace. I breathe in the scent of her shampoo mixed with fresh grass and sweat. It's intoxicating.

I pull back, suddenly aware of how close we are. "So, uh, since I missed the game... think you could give me a reenactment of your winning goal. That is if you can get it past me." I challenge.

Keely raises an eyebrow. "Oh really? You think you can block my shot?"

I laugh. "I may be injured, but I'm not dead. And I'm as good as cleared from the doctor."

She grins, a competitive glint in her eye. "Okay then. You're on, hockey boy."

We head out to the middle of the now-empty field. Keely grabs a ball from her bag and starts dribbling it between her feet.

"Alright, hotshot. Let's see what you've got," she teases.

I move towards her, careful of my knee but determined to show her I'm not completely useless. She dodges around me easily, laughing as she goes.

"Come on, Reeve! I thought you said you could keep up!"

I chase after her when she turns and starts running for the other side of the soccer field towards the other goal.

"That's cheating," I yell after her.

She squeals and then starts giggling the second she glances quickly over her shoulder to find me chasing after her.

The cool evening air fills my lungs.

For a moment, I forget about my injury, about the pressure of returning to the ice. It's just me and Keely, running and laughing under the darkening sky.

Finally, I manage to catch up to her, my arm wrapping around her waist.

She squeals again right before she loses to footing and we both tumble to the ground.

We land in a tangled heap, breathless and laughing. I find myself hovering over her, my face just inches from hers. Our laughter fades as we lock eyes.

My heart races, and I know that my self-control is wavering.

"Keely," I say softly, "I'm about to kiss you."

Her eyes widen slightly, but she doesn't pull away. Instead, her eyes dip down to my lips, and she licks her tongue and darts out to wet her bottom lip.

I start to lean in, giving her a second to deny me, but instead, she wraps her hand around the back of my neck and pulls me against her mouth.

My heart pounds against my chest as Keely pulls me closer, her lips meeting mine with unexpected intensity. The kiss deepens quickly, weeks of pent-up tension pouring out between us. Her fingers thread through my hair as my hand cups her cheek, holding her close.

I want this kiss to last longer—all night, if I had a choice, but we're in the middle of a soccer field and once we break away, I know I won't have a shot at reproducing this moment back at the apartment.

When we finally break apart, we're both breathless. I rest my forehead against hers, not wanting to put any distance between us.

"Reeve," she whispers. "It's starting to rain."

Then I feel it, a drop against the bare skin at the back of my neck. Then droplets begin to fall all around us, disappearing into the surrounding grass.

I sit up and then stand to my feet, giving Keely my hand to pull her up.

She and I stand there staring at each other for just a second and I can already see in her eyes that she knows she let down her guard. The guard she's putting back up between us.

That was it.

That was the last time I'll ever kiss Keely.

Chapter Twenty-One

Keely

It's been a few days since Reeve and I kissed on the soccer field, and next week, I'll be moving back out of the apartment since the Hawkeyes only rented the space for me for six weeks.

It seems like things are starting to wrap up from the agreement I made with Sam, Coach Bex, and Reeve. And I'm not sure how I feel about it.

I'm happy, of course, that Reeve will be back out on the ice in no time.

Having that little bit of separation might be good for us. Not living down the hall anymore will give me a reason to cut off our dinner and docu-series routine that we've fallen into. If I'm going to date Jaxson, I can't keep spending as much time with Reeve. And now that Reeve is healed up, he doesn't need me around for dinner prep or delivery.

I'm looking for a new place, but for now, I'll go back to living in my uncle's garage. Seattle's rent prices are ridiculous, and the studio apartment at my uncle's would rent for an ungodly amount, so I'm grateful to have it.

But what I need today is to hear a familiar voice. I need to talk to someone who knows all my family's dark secrets. Someone I can truly be myself with and not worry about my past coming out to ruin their lives.

I lean back in my chair, holding my phone to my ear as Paula's voice comes through. "So, tell me about this cute doctor you're going on a date with next week," she says, her tone light and teasing.

I can't help but smile, even as a twinge of guilt tugs at my heart. "His name is Jaxson. He's a surgeon at the hospital where Reeve had his surgery."

"Ooh, a surgeon. Impressive," Paula says. "And he got my girl back on the soccer field. I like him already."

"Yeah, he's really great," I admit. "He's smart, kind, and definitely easy on the eyes."

Paula chuckles. "I sense a 'but' coming."

I sigh, running a hand through my hair. There shouldn't be a 'but'. He's perfect for me, and if Reeve were nowhere in sight, I think I'd be head-over-heels for Jaxson.

"It's just... I don't know. I thought there might be something with Reeve, but..."

"But he's your patient," Paula finishes for me.

"Exactly. And even when he's not anymore, there's still the whole issue with my dad. I can't risk ruining his career. And you should meet all the amazing people in the Hawkeyes franchise. If I stay down below where no one can see me and keep my head down, there won't be an issue. But dating a player is going to draw attention. There's already a reporter doing a whole story on the Hawkeyes. She's already been asking more questions than I care to answer."

There's a pause on the other end of the line. "Keely, honey, you can't let your father's mistakes define your entire life forever. You deserve happiness too. I've never met anyone who's punished themselves for someone else's mistake harder than you have."

"I know, I know," I say, feeling the familiar weight of my family history settling on my shoulders. "It's just complicated."

"Life usually is," Paula says gently. "So, tell me more about how Reeve is doing. You must be proud of his progress."

I can't help the smile that spreads across my face. "He's doing amazing, Paula. You should see him. The doctors are talking about clearing him for practice soon."

"That's wonderful news," Paula says, and I can hear the pride in her voice. "You've done an excellent job with him, Keely. But of course, I had no doubts that you would."

Just then, my phone buzzes with a text notification. I pull it away from my ear to check it, seeing Penelope's name pop up on the screen.

> Penelope: Meet at Serendipity's at 2pm? It's time for your official initiation into the Hawkeyes girls group. I just saw an email from my dad to legal telling them to start working on your new hire contract for next week. Congratulations girlie!

> Penelope: Unrelated question: how many sticky buns do you think you could stuff in your mouth in 30 seconds or less?"

I laugh out loud, causing Paula to ask, "What's so funny?"

"Oh, just a text from one of the Hawkeyes' girlfriends. Apparently, I'm getting officially initiated into their group."

"That sounds exciting," Paula says. "You're really starting to build a life there in Seattle, aren't you?"

I pause, realizing the truth in her words. "Yeah, I guess I am."

Walking into the warm, dry coffee shop with the bright red door, I'm instantly put at ease with the soft sound of jazz music over the speakers, the smell of coffee and pastries. My eyes scan the room for a group of girls who are gathering just for the simple fact that they want to celebrate with me.

"Keely! Over here!" she calls out.

As I approach, I'm happy to see almost everyone is here. Tessa, Autumn, Brynn and Penelope and sitting together at a round oak table and chairs.

"Hi everyone," I say, sliding onto the wooden chair next to Brynn, an open seat to my right.

"We ordered you a latte," Penelope says, pushing a large mug towards me. The foam on top is artfully swirled into a leaf pattern. "Hope that's okay."

"It's perfect, thank you," I say, wrapping my hands around the warm ceramic. "So this is a real thing, huh? The girls of the Hawkeyes? And where is Isla?"

Autumn speaks up. "Yep and our membership is growing in numbers every year," she grins.

Tessa finishes her sip. "Isla texted; Berkeley has the sniffles, so she can't make it tonight," she tells me. "We're also missing Cammy who has to study for her midterms, and Juliet and Shawnie who are in Canada this weekend organizing some big celebrity wedding. They couldn't even tell us which couple."

Autumn wasn't kidding about this group growing.

"That's a lot of women inside the group. So you don't have to date a player to be invited in?" I ask, pulling my warm latte up to my lips.

Penelope's eyes twinkle, and the other girls settle back on mine. "It's not a requirement. Juliet is married to an ex-player, Shawnie works for the Hawkeyes as an event planner, and you know Cammy... she's taking over my position, and she's Seven's daughter."

"But if Penelope has her way, and she often does," Tessa chimes in. "All of them will end up as WAGS of a Hawkeyes player or coach."

I see Brynn shake her head with a smirk on her face.

"I'd be careful if I were you –trying to matchmake Cammy into the "family". Seven will lose his mind if she ends up dating a Hawkeyes player, and you know it," Brynn says.

"Well then, why am I here? I'm not dating a player, and even though you saw the paperwork, I technically haven't signed anything, so I'm not even officially an employee."

All four women look at me, calculating grins on all their faces. I'm starting to think that I was brought here under false pretenses.

"Don't worry... soon all will be revealed," Penelope says, wiggling an eyebrow, and then takes a sip of her drink.

"What does that even mean?" I ask.

Tessa rolls her eyes, annoyed with Penelope not getting to the point. "It means that Penelope, and well, all of us, think you're going to end up with Reeve."

"What?!" I practically yell.

I feel the butterflies break loose in my belly at the idea of being with Reeve and I hate that just mentioning his name does that to me.

It's incredibly inconvenient since I'm supposed to be going out with someone else next week. And because a relationship with Reeve isn't on the table.

They ignore me and move on while my brain spins. And then I feel someone sit down in the open chair next to mine.

Rowan.

"Hi girls, sorry I'm late. My tool of a boss kept all of us in a meeting that I thought would never end," she says, blowing out a breath of frustration.

"No problem, we haven't started without you," Autumn tells her.

"Okay, the initiation of the Hawkeyes Girls Club can officially commence," Penelope says with a theatrical voice.

"She's enjoying this too much," Autumn says to Brynn.

"Uh-huh," Brynn says back

Rowan bends her shoulder toward me to whisper. "I didn't know you were Oakley's niece. How come that never came up before? That's huge to the story of how Reeve met you at the bar the night you guys were in the accident. Readers are going to eat that up."

I feel a flutter of anxiety in my stomach. "Oh, um, it just never seemed relevant, I guess."

"And be honest... off the record. Are you really not dating Reeve Aisa? Because it's so obvious he has it bad for you," she whispers.

I need to squash her dreams as soon as possible. I know she wants the story with a happy ending but it's not going to happen.

"We can't date. I'm his PT... and even if I wasn't, a relationship with me could kill his career." I wince... I said too much. But maybe she'll forget it. She did say "off the record".

Tessa jumps in. "Leave the reporter act at home, Ro. We're here to celebrate Keely's new job."

Penelope pushes a plate with a sticky bun on it and a candle. She pulls a lighter out of nowhere and sets the candle ablaze.

Everyone stares at the sticky bun... no one knows what to do now.

"Are we supposed to sing to her?" Rowan asks.

Penelope shakes her head. "This is as far as we got."

"What should I do? Should I just blow out the candle?" I ask everyone in the cafe is staring and smiling at me, thinking it's my birthday.

Penelope nods.

I blow out the candle, and everyone applauds.

"How does it feel to be officially joining the Hawkeyes family?" Autumn asks.

Better than I could have ever imagined.

"Really good. Thanks, everyone," I say.

Rowan holds up a hand in question.

"Uh, okay, don't take this the wrong way but if this is a Hawkeyes girl's initiation...why am I here?" Rowan asks.

Penelope gleams over at Rowan. "Don't worry, we have plans for you next."

Chapter Twenty-Two

Keely

It's been almost a week since I got coffee with the girls.

The last few days, especially, have flown by, though I haven't seen Reeve as much as we usually do. I've been spending the days either working at Oakley's with inventory or at my uncle's helping my uncle rehab and paint the apartment above the garage.

He had new windows, updated the countertops and appliances in the tiny kitchen and replaced all the flooring with a laminate wood flooring that looks almost real.

He let me pick the paint colors and even put up a partition wall for where the bed is to make it feel less like a studio.

He didn't need to do any of that, but the project has actually been really fun to work on together, and we've bonded even more over it. By the time I make it back to the apartment at The Commons, it's usually really late and I end up passing out on the bed until the next morning.

Reeve has kept up phone calls and texts to check in, but our conversations are friendly and short. We haven't discussed what happens when I'm no longer his personal PT but instead a full-time franchise employee.

We'll still see each other--probably daily--walking through the halls--when we have our scheduled player check-in--or he needs to get taped up before a game.

But it will all be different and I can already feel it in the texts and the phone calls.

As I settle into bed, the events of the day replay in my mind. The sweet text from Jaxson confirming our date for Sunday and the restaurant that he booked. I told him after last Tuesday's game that I want to take things slow-- that I'm not interested in jumping into a relationship but that I'm open to dating casually and let things progress naturally. He agreed to my terms.

Tomorrow we hear if Reeve is cleared for light practice by the Hawkeyes doctor, and I leave my keys to this apartment and move the small amount of items I have left here back to my uncle's now that the paint fumes have mostly disappeared.

Tomorrow I go into Sam's office to sign my new contract. Sam told me yesterday that the job is mine and that hearing tomorrow about Reeve is just a formality.

Then I hear a sound coming from the floor.

The baby monitor?

I didn't realize that it had fallen down and got covered up with a pillow. Since he stopped having to ice his knee in order to sleep without the pain, I haven't needed it to check up on him.

"Keely? You there?" Reeve's voice comes through low and warm.

I hesitate for a moment, my hand hovering over the monitor. It's late and something about leaving this place tomorrow makes me feel a little emotional. I'm not sure if talking this late at night is the best option, but hearing his low bedtime voice is a guilty pleasure that I can't pass up, not when this is the last time we'll be able to use a baby monitor to chat in bed. I doubt the wave frequency of the monitors would reach my uncle's house all the way across town.

"Yeah, I'm here," I respond softly.

There's a pause, and I can almost picture him sitting on the edge of his bed, running a hand through his hair the way he does when he sits on the couch lazily watching TV with me.

"How's the apartment looking? I was going to see if I could drop by and see it today but Lake wanted to go over some new plays and then the guys all wanted to head to Oakley's for drinks," he says.

"It's looking really nice. I can breathe in the apartment without hacking at the paint fumes now. We've had to be careful about keeping too many windows open due to the moisture from all the rain. And it's been so cold that the paint doesn't want to dry as quickly."

"You move out tomorrow, right? Do you need help moving your stuff back over to Oakley's apartment?"

"That's really sweet of you to offer, but I only have a backpack left here. I've been moving everything over slowly this week."

I settle back against my pillows, pulling the comforter up to my chin. The faint glow of streetlights filters through my curtains, casting shadows across the room.

"I never heard how coffee with the girls went last week. How was that? I heard the girls are pulling Rowan into the group, too."

"It was nice," I say, trying to keep my voice steady. "They made me an honorary member of their group. And yeah, it seems Penelope has plans for her that none of us know about."

I leave out the part where they all hinted that they think Reeve and I will end up together. The memory of their knowing smiles and suggestive comments is now starting to make my heart feel a little homesick... if that even makes sense.

"That's great," Reeve says, and I can hear the genuine happiness in his voice. "I'm glad you're finding your place here."

Another pause, longer this time. I listen to the soft patter of rain against my window, waiting for him to speak again.

"Listen, Keely," he finally says, his voice softer now. It's not lost on me that he doesn't call me Doc... or Keke... or Kees. It's Keely now. "I wanted to thank you. For everything you've done to help me. I couldn't have made it this far without you."

My throat tightens at his words. "You don't have to thank me, Reeve. It's my job."

"No," he says firmly. "It's more than that. When you walked into my hospital room and they told me that you were going to be my PT, it renewed my confidence in myself and my ability despite the prognosis I was given. I'm not sure that I would have had as much faith in myself if it hadn't been you standing at my bedside, squeezing my hand."

I close my eyes, fighting back the emotions threatening to overwhelm me. "You're welcome. I'll always be on your side," I whisper.

"I know. And I'm always on yours. I want you to be happy. I hope you know that."

"I do," I say. "I agreed to go on a date with Jaxson on Sunday... I... I just thought I should tell you."

"Okay," he says simply.

The silence stretches between us, filled with unspoken words and the weight of what we can't have. I want to tell him how I feel and how much he means to me. But I know I can't. For his sake, for my sake, for the sake of his career and the team.

"Goodnight, Keely," Reeve says finally, his voice heavy with something that sounds like regret.

"Goodnight, Reeve," I respond, my voice barely audible.

I reach over and turn off the baby monitor, plunging the room into silence. As I lay in the darkness, I can't help but wonder what might have been if things were different. If I wasn't his physical therapist or if my father's past didn't hang over me like a shadow.

But as sleep finally claims me, I know that wondering about what-ifs won't change anything. Tomorrow, I'll become the Hawkeyes PT, and he and I will become co-workers...hopefully friends...but nothing more. It's all I can allow myself to be.

Chapter Twenty-Three

Reeve

I pull into the stadium parking lot, a mixture of excitement and nerves churning in my stomach. The familiar sight of the stadium feels different today. Maybe because behind those doors, I'll find the answer to the future of my career.

As I walk through the players' entrance, the cool air hits my face, carrying the faint scent of ice and sweat that I've come to associate with home. My footsteps echo in the empty corridor as I make my way toward the medical wing.

Rounding a corner, I spot two familiar figures—Keely and Cammy, deep in conversation. Keely's face lights up when she sees me, and she waves me over.

"You're here," she says, her smile warm.

"Hey," I reply, keeping my voice casual. "What are you two up to?"

Cammy grins, practically bouncing on her toes. "I'm giving Keely the official tour. She just signed as a PT for the Hawkeyes. She's a Hawkeye now."

My heart swells with pride for Keely and a sense of relief floods my chest at knowing that at least she and I will be on the same team for years to come. Even if I can't be with her the way I want to, at least I'll catch her walking through the halls. She and I will still get to work together, and that will have to be enough. "That's fantastic news," I say, pulling Keely into a quick hug. "Congratulations, you deserve it."

Keely's cheeks flush right before I release her. "Thanks, Reeve. But today's about you. Are you ready for your appointment?"

I nod, squaring my shoulders. "As ready as I'll ever be."

"You've got this," Keely says softly, giving my arm a reassuring squeeze.

"I'll be seeing you around then?" I ask over my shoulder.

"If you can find me in this place," she beams, her arms outstretched above her head.

She's dialing back her excitement because she doesn't want to overshadow my day, but in this case, her victory is mine too. Because in some small way, I still get to keep her close.

"I was the "hide and seek" reigning champ of the Juneau Boys Wilderness Camp three years in a row—don't tempt me with a good time, Doc," I say over my shoulder.

Keely's giggle echoes through the hallway and a smile tugs at the corner of my mouth.

With a deep breath, I continue down the hallway towards the doctor's office, the weight of possibility heavy on my shoulders. It's time to face the music and find out if all our hard work has paid off.

I see Coach Bex waiting by the door of Dr. Omar's office. He's waiting for me.

"You ready?" he asks.

"To get back on the ice? Yes."

Dr. Omar greets us with a warm smile, gesturing for us to take a seat. "Reeve, Coach. Good to see you both. Let's get right to it, shall we?"

I nod, my heart pounding in my chest, grateful that the doctor isn't going to meet around the bush, "Yes, please."

Dr. Omar pulls up my latest scans on his computer screen, the black and white images filling the monitor. He points to various areas, explaining in medical jargon that I barely understand. But then he turns to us, his expression serious yet optimistic.

"I'm happy to report that your knee is healing remarkably well, Reeve. The scans show significant improvement since the scans that were taken in the hospital post-surgery."

I lean forward, hardly daring to hope. "So what does that mean, Doc? Can I get back on the ice?"

Dr. Omar glances at Coach Bex and Sam before answering. "After hearing Dr. Woods' report on your recovery, and the healing that I'm seeing on your scans, I'm clearing you for light practice, effective immediately."

The words hit me like a bolt of lightning. I can feel the grin spreading across my face, my body humming with excitement.

Coach Bex speaks up, his voice gruff but pleased. "That's bloody fantastic news, Doc. But what exactly do you mean by 'light practice'?"

Dr. Omar outlines the restrictions - no contact drills, limited time on the ice, specific exercises to focus on. But I'm barely listening, already imagining the feel of my skates on the ice, the familiar weight of my gear.

As we wrap up the appointment, Coach Bex claps me on the shoulder. "Well done, mate. Now the real work begins."

I nod, determination flooding through me. "I'm ready, Coach. Let's do this."

As we leave the office, I think of who I want to tell first.

Keely.

There's no one even close. And she deserves to know first since she's the reason I'm going to be back on the ice sooner than everyone thought.

The guarantee of whether I can still play like I used to isn't assured, but that's for another day. Today, I just want to tell the one person to whom this will mean as much as it does to me.

I race through the hallways of The Commons, my heart pounding in my chest. When Dr. Omar told me I'm cleared for practice, I barely heard anything else he said. All I could think about was finding Keely, telling her the news, seeing the pride and joy on her face.

I spot her walking down the hallway, her auburn hair swaying with each step.

"Keely! Wait up!" I call out.

She stops and turns, a surprised smile spreading across her face when she sees me.

"Are you out of the meeting with the doctor already? Are you cleared?" she says, her voice questioning and excited.

I don't waste any time. I stride up to her, cupping her face in my hands. "I'm cleared," I say, my voice breathless with excitement. "Doctor said I'm good to go. I can play again."

Keely's eyes widen, her smile growing even broader, and then she wraps her hands around my wrists, keeping me close. "I knew you'd do it. I never questioned it."

The sweet inhale of her shampoo—the memory of how her lips taste against mine. I need it again, all of it—anything she'll give me.

"You've always believed in me."

The second she nods in agreement my lips crash down against hers, and it takes her a second to register my kiss but when she does, she melts into me, her hands sliding up my chest and tangling in my hair. And for a moment all I can think about is the softness of her lips, a gentle nibble she gives my lower lip and the expert way her tongue swirls against mine.

My hands trail down her body. I know her curves from the night we spent together in my bed and my shower, but I need to know more. I'm dying to memorize every inch of skin that covers her perfect body and I want her to know mine.

"You're going to get us caught," she says between our lips.

We break apart at the realization that we're out in the open, both panting slightly, desire burning in Keely's eyes. Her eyes are hooded and dilated—she wants me as badly as I want her. And though she has a date with a man I can't compete with as long as she and I both work for the Hawkeyes, she's not his yet. Not until next week.

"Come with me," I say, taking her hand.

She follows behind me, squeezing my hand tighter.

I pull her into a supply closet and lock the door, a knowing smirk on her lips when I turn back to take her mouth again.

The moment the door closes behind us, we're on each other again. Frantically discarding every inch of clothing off one another like this moment could end at any second, and we could miss our chance. I pull a condom from my wallet before my pants drop to the floor, and then, within a split second, we're pressed skin to skin.

I lift Keely up, her legs wrapping around my waist, and pin her against the wall. She lets out a soft moan as I grind against her, teasing her with my hard length.

My fingers reach for her, diving between her thighs, coating my fingers in her arousal and using it to slide my fingers in her tight pussy.

She whimpers as I ease in and out of her, my mouth swallowing every sound she makes for me. My tongue slides past her lips, claiming her fully. She tastes like heaven.

Keely kisses me back just as fiercely, her fingers threading through my hair as she keeps her thighs wrapped around my waist. I groan as our bodies meld together, her soft curves pressing against the hard planes of my chest.

"Reeve," she breathes, her head falling back against the wall.

"That's it, Keely. Let go," I growl, rocking into her harder. My fingers find her sensitive nub rubbing in tight circles. Keely cries out, her nails digging into my shoulders.

"Please... I want you," she says, and I know exactly what she wants.

I'd spend more time getting her wet, playing with her, getting her off before I give her what she's asking for, but we're in a supply closet and time isn't on our side—nothing seems to be on our side. But that won't stop me from one last time.

I roll on the condom and then notch the broad head of my cock at her entrance, thrusting into her slick heat, pulling a gasp from her lips. She's so tight, so perfect, I can barely think when she feels this fucking good.

I deepen the kiss, my tongue tangling with hers. Keely meets my passion with equal measure, her hips rolling against mine as I drive into her over and over again. The closet is filled with the sounds of our moans and the slap of skin on skin.

I can feel my release building, the familiar tightening in my lower abdomen. But I hold it back, wanting Keely to find her climax first. I redouble my efforts, my fingers finding her clit and rubbing vigorously.

"Yes, Reeve, yes!" Keely cries out, her voice high and strained. I can feel her tightening around me, her orgasm nearing.

"That's it, Keely. Come for me," I demand.

With a final thrust and a flick of my thumb, Keely shatters. Her walls clamp down around me, squeezing me like a vice as she cries out. The pulsing of her release pushes me over the edge, and I explode inside her with a guttural groan.

We stay like that for a moment, pressing against each other as we catch our breath. Finally, I lower Keely's legs back to the floor, keeping my arms around her to steady her. She looks up at me, her eyes hazy with satisfaction.

We quickly redress, stealing glances and brushes of the hands as we go. When we're presentable again, we stare back at one another, both knowing what this is but neither ready to admit it.

"That was..." she starts but trails off, seemingly at a loss for words.

"It was perfect," I finish for her, brushing a stray hair from her face.

Keely smiles, leaning into my touch. "It was," she agrees.

"And it was the last time, wasn't it?" I ask, even though I know her answer.

"It has to be."

It doesn't have to be but it's her decision.

"You slip out first. I'll give you a head start."

She nods, a somber expression across her face.

"I'm really proud of you, Reeve. I hope this doesn't take away from that."

"It doesn't. Nothing takes away from this," I say, referring to what we just did.

There's an agreement in her eyes, and then she turns to the closed door and opens it, walking out and gently closing the door behind her.

Chapter Twenty-Four

Keely

The dim lighting of the upscale restaurant that Jaxson brought me to goes a long way to help quiet my mind and settle my nerves. The first date jitters are part of it, but what really has my brain reeling is the moment Reeve and I shared in the supply closet at the Hawkeyes stadium after he was cleared by the doctor.

I'm disappointed with how easy it was for Reeve to pull me back in.

I should have been strong enough to put space between us and keep it there, but I let my emotions get in the way, and the desperate need to be with him again clouded my judgment.

I don't regret what we did.

I just regret the look on his face right before I walked out of the room, closing the door between us. And I regret that by feeding my need for one more time, my ability to think of almost anything else this whole week has been shot to hell.

At least the team has been gone the last few days for out-of-town games. I've been able to use the time to get myself setup in my new office right next door to Dr. Omar without having to see patients yet. And not having to worry about bumping into Reeve has helped me focus on my tasks.

Seeing a plaque with my name on the door each time I go to work has been the thrill of my life. And spending my lunch hour at Serendipity Coffee Shop with the girls is an unexpected perk.

"How's work going? Are you all settled into your new office?" he asks, after we've ordered our food.

The menu looks amazing, and I wish my mind hadn't drifted off to thinking that Reeve would love this place.

Maybe he's already been here before with a date?

The thought of Reeve with someone else turns my stomach but I do hope he finds someone to be happy with even though it will be painful at first to see him with someone new. But then I'll get used to it; we'll settle into a new routine and accept that our futures don't include each other. Then it will be easier to digest.

"It's better than I could have imagined. And Dr. Omar is the nicest guy. He's been filling me in on what to expect and building up my confidence for the crazy schedule I have ahead of me. I have to go through each player's chart, get caught up on their injuries and current therapy plans from the PT who's leaving, and then I have to meet with each player next week when they get home from out of town."

"Sounds like a busy schedule. I'm glad to hear that Dr. Omar is easy to work with. He seems like a good guy from the limited correspondence that he and I have had about Reeve."

My eyes drop from his and focus on the silverware on the table at the mention of Reeve's name.

I can only hope that I'm not as transparent as I feel.

"Can I ask you something?" Jaxson asks.

"Yeah, sure, anything," I tell him, my eyes finding his again.

"Did you and Reeve have a thing for each other?"

"A thing? Reeve and me? Why do you ask?"

I already feel outed but confessing that Reeve and I hooked up while he was my PT patient is not something I'll be giving up freely.

"Because what I've heard about Reeve is that he's one of the nicest hockey players on the team, but I can tell he doesn't care for me much and I can't think of anything I've done besides pull off a difficult surgery to save his career."

I'm relieved that he's asking because he thinks he sees the desire to be together in Reeve's eyes... and not because he just caught it in mine.

"What do you mean? He usually seems pleasant around you whenever I've seen you two interact."

"Yeah... at face value. But then I see his shoulders tense and his jaw tighten."

"I think you're seeing things," I chuckle, trying to lighten the mood.

I haven't witnessed any of that, but I can't promise that Jaxson is seeing things. He could be reading Reeve correctly.

"I'm a doctor. I'm acutely aware when someone I see has a muscle tic. And Reeve seems to only have one when I'm standing near you. It's an occupational hazard to notice things about people. It could save a life if I can diagnose a health issue quickly."

"What do you see when you see me?" I ask, laying down my fork and resting my hand on my chin with my elbow on the table.

"You're attracted to me," he says with a sexy smile, and then it falters slightly. "But you're playful with him. He puts you at ease. An ease that I don't usually see you in, not at Oakley's, not on the soccer field, and not with me."

It seems he sees more than a doctor looking for health concerns, but he's not wrong.

"I've spent more time with him than I've spent with you. I'm easier around people and places I know well."

"Okay, I'll accept that. But why are you tense at your uncle's bar that you know well or on a soccer field which you seem to know better than half the players on the city league combined?"

Okay, he might have a point.

Being around Reeve does something to me. I can't deny that.

Maybe it's because I feel safe with him?

But I can't admit any of that to Jaxson because then he'll think there is something going on between Reeve and me, that isn't.

I like Jaxson—a lot, actually.

We have a lot in common, like the medical field, soccer, and shithead dads.

It also doesn't hurt his case that my uncle really likes him, which can be a hard sell—and he's a hot surgeon.

"I think it's just that large crowds make me uneasy. I'm always worried that someone in the sports world is going to find out who I'm related to and judge me for it. Which is also why I can promise you that nothing would ever happen between me and Reeve. It would kill his career."

His eyebrows raise. "That's a heavy statement. Plenty of us have shitty parents. What's so great about yours that they would end up killing a highly-ranked NHL goalie's career?" he asks

He pulls his water glass toward him and then takes a sip.

I take a deep breath. I don't exactly want to admit this to him but at the same time... I feel like I might explode if I don't tell someone. And besides, if this relationship is going to continue, he's going to find out soon enough. I can't keep my history from someone I'm seeing seriously, forever.

And if this thing with Jaxson turns into forever, will he be mad when I tell him that my uncle Oakley is going to walk me down the aisle instead of my dad? Since my dad spent most of my life in prison? Especially because Jaxson was so open about his family with me.

No, I should just tell him now and get the secrets out of the way.

"My dad used to work for the mob," I say.

"Oh..." Jaxson pulls back in surprise. "I wasn't expecting that. Maybe your family situation is worse than mine," he says with a polite chuckle.

"Yeah..." I nod, reaching for my wine glass.

I swirl the last of the red liquid in my glass, watching as it glides close to the rim.

"I could see how that could be considered tabloid catnip but I don't think it would even make it to the front page. And I don't see how it would end Reeve's career."

"I'll tell you, but first, I would like to request special doctor/patient privileges before I continue."

Jaxson puts down his fork and reaches out for my free hand lying on the table.

"You're not my patient but you have my word that I won't tell a soul."

His eyes soften as they gaze into mine and I believe that he'll keep my secret. I just hope that I'm not making a mistake by telling him.

"Do you remember the scandal around the World Cup fifteen years ago?" I ask.

"Of course I do. Back then I was going into my freshman year of high school and thought I was going to be a professional soccer player. A lot changed for me the next day when I found out that we lost the house. After that, soccer left a bad taste in my mouth."

"Yeah, well everything around me crumbled after that night too when the FBI broke through the front door with a SWAT team and pulled my dad out of our house."

"Oh shit..." he says, squeezing my hand. "That must have been terrifying—being so young and having that happen."

"It was."

I nod, remembering the bright light of high-powered swat flashlights shining under my bedroom door. But no one opened it to tell me what was going on.

"That's my daughter's room. Don't go in there," he threatened whoever was pulling him through the house as they passed by my room. I wasn't supposed to be there that night but my mom had to fly out of town to see a great aunt in Florida so I got to stay with my dad for the entire weekend.

My mother resented him for putting us through hell. From the night they broke through the front door while I was staying with him, to the year-long criminal trial, to the death threats from of Soccer fans from all around the world that came to our mailbox for *years*.

She refused to let fear move us out of town even though my uncle Oakley begged her to move me to Seattle and out of Mesa. But her family and friends were still there, we still had support from so many.

"What happened next," he asks.

"My father stood trial for his involvement in the World Cup racketeering scandal."

Jaxson's face falls and his skin turns gray. He pulls his hand off mine slowly—my skin losing his heat with each inch he pulls back until I'm left cold again, like I have been for the last fifteen years.

"Fuck..." he mutters to himself and stares down at his lap.

Though I'm not usually surprised by his reaction... It's usually not people in the medical field that take the news this hard. I had told a few people in college when the conversation came up over late-night study parties. People's eyes would widen but more to the fact that my dad was in the mob. The World Cup didn't mean much to most of them, and not many even remember hearing about the scandal.

It's one of the reasons I stayed in school and got my doctorate instead of stopping at my master's. College was the first time that I felt safe with my peers. People were too damn busy trying to juggle exams, coursework, extra school credit, additional lab time, and a mountain of school debt to care about anyone else's life problems other than their own.

It was more like, *"Oh... your dad is a convicted mobster who paid a whole team of players to throw one of the highest televised sporting events of all time? Great.... Now, can I borrow your notes from the anatomy lecture from yesterday?"*

Those years were the happiest I had ever been since I was fourteen.

When Jaxson doesn't say anything, I continue.

"My dad just got out recently, and if Reeve and I started dating, then it could look bad on sponsorships and teams looking to take him on as a player. No one will want to associate with a player whose girlfriend is linked to a guy who paid off a team to throw a game. No one will believe that my father isn't out of prison and still working for the mob, trying to convince Reeve to throw a hockey game. He'll become too much of a risk for teams to take on."

Jaxson's eyes are still cast down—deep in thought—or shock. I'm not sure which.

"Keely," he says, peering up, his eyes full of emotion. "Jesus, I can't believe I'm about to say this. It's been a really long time since I've felt this way about anyone. I started thinking that you could turn out to be the... never mind, that's not helpful right now."

I didn't finish the sentence, but I can guess.

He started thinking that I could turn out to be the *one*.

We're not even together and he's breaking up with me over my father's transgression.

Figures. Life keeps playing a cruel joke on me, but no one seems to be laughing.

"It's fine. You don't have to say anything. I'm used to this reaction by now. We can split the check, and I'll call a rideshare to take me home," I say, reaching up a hand to flag down the waitress.

"Wait—Split the check?—Get a rideshare?" he says, holding up a hand to stop me. "You caught me off guard. Just give me a second to wrap my brain around this."

I sit back against my chair, pulling my hands off the table and pull my arms around my waist protectively.

"Do you remember how I told you that my mother divorced my father after he lost our house because he gambled the note away?" I nod, the story coming back to my memory. "And do you remember how I told you that my dad is a bigger soccer fan than me and always dreamed I'd play professionally?" I nod again. "Keely, he bet our house on the World Cup and lost. That was the bet that cost me my family."

I let out a shaky breath.

So many of the death threats we received were from people who had lost money on the game. People who lost their families like Jaxson did because they bet their life savings, retirement, children's college funds, or other assets. And though I won't defend my father's actions, it's impossible to know which team would have won that night if it hadn't been fixed. All those people would have lost anyway if the team my dad paid off did win the game that night.

"I'm sorry that happened to you, Jaxson. I really am," I say, my eyes darting away from him and down at my half-eaten meal, which I'm no longer hungry enough to eat.

He runs a hand through his hair and blows out a breath.

"It's not your fault. I don't blame you for what your father did or for the detrimental decisions my father made that led to our family imploding—in my father's case, it would have happened eventually. But the thing is... I'll never be able to introduce you to my mom. My parents just barely got back on speaking terms, agreeing to a ceasefire for my brother's wedding. Bringing you into the mix now will stir up old hurt that she's finally buried for my brother's sake."

My father's sins strike again.

I can't hide the disappointment and hurt on my face.

"This hurts me more than it will hurt you," he says.

I cock an eyebrow at him. "Why would you say that?"

"Because he's been waiting, hoping I'll step out of line, and the minute I do, he's going to step in to fill my spot."

Step in to fill his spot?

"Who?"

His eyes soften toward me. There are no hard feelings in his eyes—just matched disappointment.

"You know who."

Chapter Twenty-Five

Reeve

I pull up to Oakley's house, my heart racing as I park behind Keely's car and glance up the stairs nestled against the garage that I assume lead to her studio apartment. With the cold, overcast fall day, it's nice to see the warm glow of the lights on in her apartment.

It's been a couple of days since the team and I arrived back from our away games. I've been meaning to make it over here sooner but with me back on the ice, I've been training as much as Coach Bex will allow and then I'm back to my apartment to ice my knee. It still swells up after a long day of practice, but I'll take a freezing ice pack, over warming a bench any day.

"Hey there," I hear Oakley call out, standing on a ladder and scooping out leaves from his house gutters. "Are you here to see Keely?"

"Yeah. And I bought that TV you told me she didn't have. Can you help me take it up the stairs?" I ask.

"On my way," he says and starts coming down the ladder.

While out of town I had a nagging feeling that I needed to do something for her new apartment. A housewarming present—a "congrats on the new job" gift—a "thank you for getting me back on the ice"... I wanted to get her something big enough to cover all of that. I knew if I asked her what she needed for the apartment, she'd tell me not to spend my money, but I have more money than I can spend and she deserves it. So I went over her head and asked Oakley what she still needed for the apartment.

He said that she doesn't have a TV yet and since I know she likes those documentaries that we watch together, I figured it was the best choice. Plus, with a TV, it's not like trying to pick out a couch for her— it's not likely I'll pick the wrong size, color or style.

Smart TV—black—flatscreen— sixty inches... done.

The stairs creak slightly under our feet as we ascend up the stairs, me walking backward all the way up while Oakley follows behind, gripping the other end of the television box.

"Had to buy the biggest one you could find, huh?" he says with a playful huff.

It's not heavy and not even close to the biggest TV in the store. It might be big for a studio apartment, but I wanted it to be big enough for her to see from her bed. Though I just about drop my side of the TV when I think about Jaxson being in that bed with her.

We finally make it up to the landing and it's surprisingly big enough for me and the TV but not Oakley.

"I got it from here if you want to get back to your project before it starts raining again. Thanks for your help," I tell him, knowing that I can pull the TV into the apartment the rest of the way.

"No problem. And hey, I'm throwing my annual Thanksgiving dinner at Oakley's. Seven, Lake, and the girls are coming along with some friends—should be a good turnout. We've got room if you want to come by."

"I might take you up on that."

He pats the TV box and then turns to head back down the stairs.

I hesitate for a moment before knocking, my knuckles rapping softly against the wooden door. There's a shuffling sound from inside, and then the door swings open.

Keely stands there, her auburn hair in a messy bun and wearing comfortable clothes - yoga pants and... my hoodie. I didn't realize that she still had it.

Her eyes go wide in surprise, pulling my hoodie up higher around her neck as a chill breeze whips past us and through the door "Reeve? What are you doing here?"

I can't help but smile at her reaction. "Hey, Doc. I wanted to see your new place. And I brought you something."

I gesture at the large TV box next to me.

"You bought me a giant TV?" she asks, staring down at the box, her eyebrow arched.

"Oakley said you didn't have one and I didn't want you missing out on any of that series we've been watching."

She steps back, gesturing for me to come in. "That was really thoughtful, thank you. Do you need help with that?"

There's a handle cut out on the side of the box, so I slide my hand in and pull it with me through her door.

"No, I got it."

The apartment is small but cozy. The scent of fresh paint lingers in the air, mixed with a hint of vanilla - probably from the candle flickering on a nearby shelf. I take in the space, noticing how she's already made it her own with a few personal touches.

I take notice of the bed in the corner, tucked behind one wall. The bed is made so there's no way to see if both sides are being used. The one thing I do notice that stands out? The baby monitor is perched on one of the end tables.

"This is nice," I say, turning back to face her. "How are you settling in?"

Keely shrugs, a small smile playing on her lips. "It's coming along. And it's a perfect spot since it's just me."

"Just me."

The words hang in the air between us. I want to ask if "just me" is because she's the only one who lives here? Or if it means also that no one comes to visit. Like soccer-playing surgeons who can't keep their eyes off of her.

We chat for a few minutes about work and the team, but there's an underlying tension that wasn't there before. It's like we're both hyper-aware of every word, every movement. I can't keep my attention off of her in my hoodie.

"What?" she asks when she sees me staring at the way the sweatshirt swallows her up.

"You still have it," I say, gesturing to the black hoodie with the Hawkeyes team logo over the front.

"Oh..." She glances down at the baggy material. "I forgot I was wearing this. It's the most comfortable thing in my closet," her eyes flash up to mine. "You probably want it back."

She reaches to pull it off her body but I put my hand against her arm to stop her.

"No, it's fine. Keep it. It was my backup, and I like knowing that you wear it."

She seems relieved to not have to give it back to me and I like the idea of her wrapped up in something of mine.

Finally, I remember the other thing I brought with me. I pull the baby monitor out of my jacket pocket. "I almost forgot. I wanted to return this to you."

Keely looks at the monitor, then back at me. A mischievous glint appears in her eye. "You know what? Why don't you keep it? As a memento of our time together."

I raise an eyebrow. "A memento?"

She laughs, the sound warming me from the inside out. "Yeah, you know. To remember your time as my patient. Your journey back to the ice."

I turn the monitor over in my hands, remembering all the late-night conversations we had through it. All the times her voice comforted me when the pain was bad. "Is that why your monitor is still sitting on your nightstand?"

She whips her head over toward the bedroom. "Oh... I didn't even know I put it there. I must have set it there while I was unpacking and didn't think about what I was doing."

She did it subconsciously. She automatically thought to keep it close by her bedside. "Right. Thanks, Keeks. I'll keep it safe."

We stand there for a moment, the silence stretching between us. I can hear the faint ticking of a clock somewhere in the apartment, marking the passing seconds.

"Well," I finally say, "I should probably get going. Let you get back to settling in."

Keely nods, walking me to the door. "Thanks for stopping by Reeve. And for the monster-sized TV."

I twist the knob on the front door and step out. It's only sixty inches. The TV in my apartment would eat hers for breakfast. "It's not that big," I say.

"Don't sell yourself short, Aisa," she teases with a wink, leaning against the door.

As I step outside, the cool evening air hits my face. I turn back to her, taking in her silhouette framed by the warm light from inside. "There's nothing short about it. I'll see you around?"

She smiles softly. "Yeah, I'll see you around."

As I walk back to my car, the baby monitor feels heavy in my pocket. A memento, she called it.

I climb into my car and sit there for a moment, staring at the lit window of Keely's apartment. With a sigh, I start the engine and drive away.

It never gets easier leaving her behind.

The drive back to the apartment had my head reeling and the only thing that helps when I need to work through something, is to skate. I pull into the Hawkeyes parking lot instead.

It's late when I push through the doors of the stadium, the cleaning crew making their usual rounds.

I notice Coach Bex's light is still on in his office as I pass by, then I see a familiar face coming out of his office and slamming it as she exits.

Rowan.

She doesn't see me yet and she mumbles a string of curse words.

"Ms. Summers," I call out.

She looks up in shock to see me on the other side of the hallway.

"Reeve, I didn't think anyone else was here tonight."

"You okay? T-Rex swinging around those short little arms again?" I ask.

She chuckles and then shakes her head and rolls her eyes. "He's impossible. We'll never see eye to eye because he refuses to believe that I'm not looking for a hidden angle."

"Is he right?" I ask.

Her eyes search mine for a second. "Can I ask you something?"

"Is it off the record?" I tease, though I'd like everything to stay off the record.

"Oh, this is so far off the record it will never see the light of day as long as I have something to say about it. But I think you'll want to know, and since you were candid with me about Coach Bex a while back, I feel like I owe it to tell you."

I don't like the fact that her smile fades. Whatever this is, it doesn't sound good.

"Do you know who Oakley Humphries' brother is? Barrett Humphries?" she asks.

"Barrett who?"

I know Oakley has mentioned that he had one brother but as far as I know, they don't talk and he's been in prison for years, though I don't think I ever heard of the reason why.

"I started digging into Keely's background and her family. My boss thinks that the story of you saving Keely and then her becoming your PT is the feel-good story that he wants out in front of the longer story I'm doing about the Hawkeyes. But when I looked her up, all the basic stuff came up—where she went to high school, where she got her doctorate and the ACL she tore in middle school. Most reporters would have enough to use to fill their quota but then I heard that Humphries is the family name, not Woods."

It just now dawns on me that Rowan is right... Keely's last name is Woods, not Humphries. But if Keely is the daughter of Oakley's brother, she would have the Humphries name.

"Leave Keely alone," I tell her.

Whatever information she found, she needs to un-find it because I don't like the way Rowan is looking at me.

"I'm just doing my job, Reeve."

"Then stop doing it," I say, pushing past her, back down toward the hall.

"Keely's dad is the same man who did fifteen years for racketeering the World Cup for the mob—Barrett Humphries. Woods is her mother's name," she calls out behind me.

I stop and turn back toward her. "That was her dad? Keely told you this?"

"No, but she told me at Serendipity's Coffee Shop with the girls that a relationship with her could kill your career."

"She said that?"

Keely suggesting that we can't date because of us working together never made sense. She knew that the Hawkeyes don't care about people inside the organization dating as long as HR knows about it and there was always a part of me that thought there might have been something more to it than what she was telling me.

Rowan nods. "And I thought she was exaggerating until I did a lot of digging. No other reporter would have found this out. If you ask me, a lot of the information was erased about her dad. I couldn't have figured it out without knowing Oakley's last name and Keely prompting me to dig deeper," she says. "It might be my best work yet."

"Rowan—" I warn.

"Don't worry. No one will figure this one out and I have no plans of telling a soul except you."

"Why only me?"

"Because these girls are becoming my friends and I will protect each of them for as long as I can... and because it's obvious to me that Keely is holding herself back from being with you, and I believe this is the real reason why."

"How do you know that she wants to be with me?"

I want her to tell me that Keely confessed it all to her, but I know that's pushing my luck. Though I'm furious about Keely for keeping us apart for this reason, I'll be relieved if this is the thing keeping us apart.

"I'm a reporter Aisa, I look for the things people don't want me to find... like their true feelings."

Chapter Twenty-Six

Thanksgiving

Reeve

The rich aroma of roasted turkey and savory stuffing wafts through Oakley's as I push open the front door of the bar.

The place is buzzing with conversation and laughter from familiar faces. Strings of twinkling lights are draped across the ceiling, casting a soft glow over the room and giving it a cozy, festive atmosphere.

I scan the crowd, my eyes searching for one person in particular. When I spot Keely setting up a long table that looks like it could seat at least forty people, my heart skips a beat. She's wearing a burgundy sweater that brings out the warmth in her eyes, and her long hair cascades down her back in loose waves as tendrils frame her face.

As I make my way over, I notice Seven and Brynn arranging place settings while Brent and Tessa are carefully placing centerpieces along the table. Lake is helping Oakley carry in more chairs from the back.

"Hey," I say, approaching Keely. "Need a hand?"

She looks up, a smile spreading across her face. "I didn't know you were coming. Yeah, sure, could you help me with these napkins?"

As we work, each of us takes a stack and lays a napkin, perfectly pre-folded onto each plate around the place setting; I look around and notice that someone I was expecting to see is missing.

"Where's Jaxson? I thought he might be here."

Keely's hands pause for a moment before resuming their task. "Oh, I don't know. He's probably on call tonight. That would be my guess."

I try to keep my voice neutral, but her lack of knowledge about where the man she's dating is on a major holiday seems odd. "You don't know where your boyfriend is?"

She doesn't look up across the table as she continues her task, dropping the last couple of napkins down. "He's not my boyfriend. We're not dating."

They're not dating? Didn't they go on their first date?

Before I can ask her to clarify, Tessa and Brynn approach us, both grinning.

"Keely, where do you want us to put the glasses and silverware?" Tessa asks.

"Oh, um, maybe over by the bar for now? We can bring them over once the table's set," Keely suggests.

As the girls head off to follow her instructions, I try to catch Keely's eye again, but we're interrupted by Oakley's booming voice.

"Alright, everyone! Turkey's ready. Let's get this feast started."

The next few minutes are a flurry of activity as dishes are brought out and everyone finds their seats. I end up sitting across from Keely, with Seven on one side of me and Brent on the other. The table is laden with golden-brown turkey, mountains of mashed potatoes, boats of gravy, and every side dish imaginable.

Once everyone is seated, Oakley stands, clinking his glass with a fork to get our attention. The room falls silent as all eyes turn to him.

"Before we dig in," he begins, his voice warm and full of emotion, "I'd like to propose a toast. This year, I'm grateful for many things, but most of all, I'm grateful for family —both old and new."

His eyes find Keely, and I see her smile softly.

"I'm thankful for Keely moving closer, and for the Hawkeyes family who have given her a reason to stay," Oakley continues. Then, to my surprise, he turns to me. "And to Reeve, for also keeping my girl safe."

I feel a flush creep up my neck as Keely and I make brief eye contact before she quickly looks away.

As Oakley sits down, I feel compelled to stand. All eyes turn to me, and I clear my throat. I'm not one who suffers from stage fright, if I did, I wouldn't have picked to play professional hockey, but there's a lot riding on me getting this right.

"I, uh, I'd also like to say something if that's alright," I begin. "I'm thankful to be cleared to be back on the ice. I'm grateful for a great team who has had my back through some tough moment," I say, looking to my right and then to my left at my Seven and Brent, "and I'm thankful this year for another chance to take our team to the playoffs." Seven, Brent and Lake all sound off in agreement. "but mostly..." I pause, my eyes finding Keely's across the table. "I'm grateful for Keely. Not only for giving everything she had to get me back on the ice... but for being the unwavering support I never knew I needed. You've become an essential part of my life, my best friend. Your strength and compassion have inspired me, and I can't imagine facing the challenges ahead without you by my side. I love you."

Keely's eyes widen and she abruptly pushes back from the table, her chair scraping against the floor as she stands.

"Excuse me," she mumbles, rushing towards the back of the bar.

Without thinking, I follow her, ignoring the curious glances from our friends. I find her in the hallway leading to the restrooms, her back to me as she leans against the wall.

"Keely?" I say softly, approaching her. "Are you okay?"

She turns to face me, her eyes shimmering with unshed tears. "Reeve, I... I can't do this."

"Do what?" I ask, taking a step closer.

"This," she gestures between us. "Pretending like there's nothing between us when clearly there is."

My heart races at her words. "Then stop pretending and be with me," I say, reaching for her hand.

She shakes her head, but she doesn't let go. "We can't."

"Why? Because you think no one will want to touch me just because of who your dad is?"

Keely's eyes widen in shock, but I press on before she can speak.

"Wait... how do you know about that?"

"I can't reveal my sources, but I wish you would have told me sooner. Is this the real reason that you've been pushing me away?"

She looks away not wanting to admit to it, but her lack of words confirm what Rowan suspected.

"Listen to me, Keely. What your father did was fifteen years ago. It's old news. The sports world has moved on, and so should you."

She shakes her head, tears threatening to spill. "You don't understand. It could still affect your career, your sponsorships-"

I cup her face in my hands, forcing her to look at me. "I don't care about any of that. If it becomes an issue, which I highly doubt it will, I'll deal with it—we'll deal with it, together. I can always find somewhere to skate, Keely. But I can't find another you."

"Reeve..." she whispers, her resolve wavering.

"I love you, Keely. All of you. Your past, your present, your future. I want it all, and if you would have been honest with me in the beginning, I would have told you that. I'm willing to face whatever comes our way, but no more keeping things from me. We're a team now."

I can see the conflict in her eyes, the battle between her fears and her feelings.

"But what if-" she starts, but I cut her off.

"No more 'what ifs'. I'm here, right now, telling you that I choose you. Your father's mistakes don't define you, and they certainly don't change how I feel about you."

Keely's eyes search mine, looking for any hint of doubt. Finding none, she lets out a shaky breath.

"I love you too, Reeve," she admits, her voice thick with emotion. "I've been trying so hard not to, but I can't fight it anymore."

Without another word, I pull her close and press my lips to hers. The kiss is desperate and filled with all the pent-up emotions we've been holding back. Keely's arms wrap around my neck as she melts into me, and I hold her tight, pouring everything I feel for her into this moment.

When we finally break apart, I gaze into her eyes, and I gently stroke her cheek.

"No more running?" I ask softly.

"No more running," she agrees.

As we stand there, wrapped in each other's arms, I feel truly thankful for everything that's led us to this moment.

Epilogue

Keely

"It's been two years today since the night of the accident," I tell Reeve, lying in bed in our new, bigger apartment at The Commons while he scrolls through YouTube to find the series we've been watching from a vlogger who travels around all the most barren or desolate areas of the earth to discover the tribes or colonies that still live there. In this next episode, he's supposed to be in Siberia.

He's home for a couple more days with the Hawkeyes until they head back out on the road for four nights.

Though his prognosis didn't look good after the night of the accident, Reeve worked his butt off and was cleared the week before Christmas to play again. Dr. Morgan was in the stands that night, wearing an AISA jersey... and so was I.

"You think of it as the night I got hit by that car?" he asks, still scrolling through our 'favorites' list where we've kept it since he's been out of town on games and we haven't gotten to watch it yet.

The driver was finally caught... oddly enough, by my uncle who drove around town for months on end finally did result in the discovery of a car parked at a body shop to get fixed.

It turns out that it wasn't a drunk driver at all, but a seventeen-year-old kid who took his parents' expensive luxury car out for a joy ride when they were out of town and dropped his cell phone right before we walked out into the crosswalk. He told his parents he hit a deer.

The reason he gave for not stopping—he got scared after seeing me and Reeve laid out on the asphalt so he took off. Then when the media got ahold of the story, he was too scared to come forward due to the backlash.

"Yeah... what do you think of it as?"

His eyes turn down to me, tucked at his side, my body plastered against his— my leg curling around his thigh as I try to get as close as physically possible.

"The night I met you."

I can't help the wide grin I give him.

He bends down and kisses me.

"I love you, Keely.

"I love you too.

Then his attention moves back to the YouTube channel.

"Oh look, he's live tonight," Reeve says, and clicks on the video.

As the livestream begins, we see the familiar face of the travel vlogger, bundled up against the Siberian cold. He's standing in front of a vast, snow-covered landscape, his breath visible in the frigid air.

"Hello, viewers! We're coming to you live from the heart of Siberia," he begins, his voice slightly crackly through our phone speakers. "But before we dive into today's adventure, I have a special message for two of our most dedicated viewers."

My heart skips a beat as I glance up at Reeve, but his eyes are fixed on the screen, a small smile playing at the corners of his mouth.

The vlogger continues, "Keely and Reeve, this one's for you." He reaches into his pocket and pulls out a small velvet box. "Reeve asked me to help him with something very important tonight."

Suddenly, I feel Reeve shift beside me. He sits up, gently pulling me with him, and takes my hands in his.

"Keely," Reeve says. "Two years ago, our lives changed forever. What could have been the worst night of my life became the best, because it brought you to me. Every day since then, you've shown me what true strength and love look like. When people say to make sure and marry your best friend, I never knew what they meant until I met you."

Tears well up in my eyes as Reeve reaches for something on the nightstand – an identical velvet box to the one on screen. He opens it, revealing a beautiful ring that glimmers in the soft light of our bedroom.

"Will you marry me?" Reeve asks.

Overwhelmed with emotion, I throw my arms around Reeve's neck, nodding vigorously. "Yes!" I manage to choke out between happy sobs. "Yes, of course I will!"

As Reeve slips the ring onto my finger, we embrace in a kiss, a kiss that means forever.

THE END

Thank you for reading Tough Score!

To read the next book, Perfect Score, you can find it on Amazon or on my website.

Keep up with Kenna by following here:

Printed in Dunstable, United Kingdom